Love
TAKES ALL

J. M. Jeffries

HARLEQUIN® KIMANI™ ROMANCE

To the next generation: Frederik, Kathryn and baby Pace (about to arrive in the world), may you each find your heart's desire.

Recycling programs
for this product may
not exist in your area.

ISBN-13: 978-0-373-86354-9

LOVE TAKES ALL

For questions and comments about the quality of this book please contact us at CustomerService@Harlequin.com.

HARLEQUIN®
www.Harlequin.com

Printed in U.S.A.

Dear Reader,

Life's a gamble. You have to know when to play the hand dealt you or throw it in and start over. You need to know when to take action and when to stand back. On the turn of a card, you can win a casino or lose a fortune. Reno, Nevada, may lack the luster of Vegas, but at heart it's still a rip-roaring frontier town.

Lydia Montgomery has spent her life bending to the will of others and now she has a chance to start over. As part owner in the Mariposa Hotel and Casino, she is hungrily looking toward her future. Hunter Russell is reluctant to take risks, but when his grandmother needs him, he puts aside everything and joins her in Reno.

Join Lydia and Hunter as they deal the cards and win at the game of love.

Much love,

Jackie and Miriam

J.M. Jeffries

Jeff and Erin, Miriam and Peter, you make beautiful grandbabies. Thank you for all the riches and love you bring to me. Mom.

To my wonderful family: Thank you for your love, support and patience. Love, Jackie.

Prologue

Lydia Montgomery sat in the darkened gallery leaning slightly forward to peer through the clear glass at the poker table below. Lydia was just one of a few people left watching the private poker game.

She clutched the arm of her chair, trying to stay calm. Miss Eleanor Russell, looking cool and collected as always, sat at the poker table. Her back was ramrod straight. Her beautiful gray hair was in a lovely upswept style that gave her such elegant air Lydia was almost jealous. Lydia had been trained from an early age to be elegant. For her it was sometimes a challenge, but for Miss Eleanor it was effortless.

Lydia smoothed the cool silk fabric of her black pants and tugged at her Arctic white turtleneck. The room was cold, kept icy so the poker players stayed alert. Only one other person remained at the poker table, besides Miss E. and the dealer. Only one person stood between Lydia and her new life. She wanted to send the evil mojo toward him like nobody's business, but since she had been raised to be a lady, she could only think about doing it.

The other player sat slumped over his cards, his face hidden behind large sunglasses. He kept his cards face down on the table while the dealer dealt another card.

"Are you watching him?" Jasper Biggins leaned over

to whisper to Lydia. He was in his mid-sixties with iron gray hair and strong hands. His blue eyes held a twinkle. He told her he'd lived in Reno his whole life.

Miss E. had told Lydia he owned this beautiful casino with a twelve-story hotel rising overhead. Why Jasper wanted to be rid of the *Casa de Mariposa* was a mystery to Lydia, though Miss E. probably knew. Miss E. knew everything. And she wasn't telling.

"What am I looking for?" She studied man, hoping she would see his tell. Behind him, at the opposite end of the gallery, a woman sat watching the game with the same level of concentrated interest as Lydia. She vaguely remembered being told the woman was Jasper's daughter. She was a slender, brittle-looking woman with a hard face and angry eyes.

The pile of chips in front of the man at the poker table was considerably smaller than it had been at the beginning of the game, when the last seven players out of the original seventy-seven sat down to try their luck in winning the casino, the final prize of the game.

"Watch his hands." Jasper pointed a bony finger, directing her gaze to the player below.

Lydia leaned forward and realized the man sitting across from Miss E. clutched his fingers tightly. A few minutes earlier they had been more relaxed.

"That's his tell," Jasper said. "I don't think he even realizes what he's doing."

Most professional players thought their eyes and facial expressions gave them away, hence the oversized sunglasses to hide what he thought must be his tell. Jasper had been educating Lydia, giving her a running commentary on the game as it progressed. Lydia had a rudimentary knowledge of the game learned at Miss E.'s poker school when Lydia had first attended. But Jasper brought a deeper, more profound knowledge of the game and Lydia was happy to listen.

Miss Eleanor tapped the table, her long graceful fingers holding her cards almost daintily. She wore clear reading glasses, her own face impassive. If she had a tell, Lydia hadn't spotted it yet. Miss E. looked completely unassuming and harmless, yet Lydia knew a tigress lurked beneath that tranquil, serene exterior.

The dealer slid a card toward Miss E. and she smiled at him and said thank-you. She was always gracious, always mannerly while the other player tended to be surly. The man shoved all the stacks of chips in front of him to the center of the table. Eleanor matched it.

Lydia believed Miss E. had her opponent on the run, but Lydia had been taking poker lessons for only the past few months, so she wasn't quite sure what was going on. Miss Eleanor had taught Lydia the mechanics of poker, but the more subtle details of the game eluded her.

Miss Eleanor's opponent said something. Miss Eleanor raised a delicate eyebrow. Slowly she turned over the cards in front of her, not even looking at them. With an angry twist to his lips, the man threw his cards at her and stood up. Miss Eleanor smiled and scooped up all the chips and the deed for the casino that had been the final prize. Miss Eleanor had won.

Lydia tilted her head at Miss Eleanor. "Lydia," she said in a clear voice, "you, Reed and I are now the proud owners of the *Casa de Mariposa*."

Lydia wet her lips. "I knew you wouldn't lose." Her nervousness drained away, replaced by elation. She had set out to do something different with her life, and here she was a former upper crust hostess of New Orleans society and now the new owner of a casino.

Miss. E. leaned close to the window, her voice carried

into the gallery by a microphone. "You can take a breath now, sweetie."

Lydia did. She jumped to her feet. She couldn't wait to tell Maya.

"Let's go enjoy our victory." Jasper held out a hand to her.

Across the gallery Jasper's daughter watched them, her mouth tight with anger. She glared at her father, then turned on her heel and left the gallery.

"Of course." Lydia gathered up her purse and jacket and headed toward the gallery door, Jasper following on her heels.

In the hall outside the poker room, Miss Eleanor handed the signed deed to Lydia. "I'm going to call Reed. I wish he could have been here. He'll be ecstatic."

Lydia had yet to meet Reed. He'd been called home to deal with a family emergency.

She stared at the deed, excited, scared and hopeful. She could hardly wait to go back to her suite to tell her daughter. Their new life in Reno, Nevada, had just begun.

Chapter 1

Hunter Russell woke and tried to figure out what was ringing. Darkness outside the windows of his apartment told him it was still night. A quick glance at the clock told him it was just after three a.m. A few sleepy moments passed before he realized the ringing sound was his phone. He grabbed the device, feeling a surge of worry when he saw his grandmother's number on the display. His heart started racing as panic engulfed him.

"Miss E," he said, "what's wrong? Are you okay?" Dire thoughts rushed through him.

She laughed. "I'm fine, Hunter. Just fine. Nothing is wrong."

In his experience, phone calls at three a.m. were never good. "Then why are you calling?" He sat up, struggling to push sleep away. If nothing was wrong, why was his seventy-eight-year-old grandmother calling at three in the morning?

"Pack your bags, Hunter, I need you in Reno. Immediately."

Lingering drowsiness finally cleared. "Are you sure you're okay? Are you sure you're not ill?"

"Trust me. Everything is fabulous," she said, still laughing. "I just won a casino in a poker game."

"You what?"

She repeated her statement, pausing between each word. "I…just…won…a…casino. In a poker game."

He shook his head. Had he heard her right? "Did you just say you won a casino?"

"Twice, Hunter. Wake up."

That wasn't what he expected to hear. "Miss E., are you insane? Are you drunk?"

"Grandson," she said sharply, "do you think I can't reach through this phone and slap you upside the head?"

Hunter tried not to flinch. He did think that. His grandmother was capable of anything. "I'm sorry, Miss E. Just start from the beginning and talk really slow."

She sighed. "I had an opportunity to win a casino in a poker game. Lydia Montgomery and Reed Watson staked me and I won that baby on an inside straight that no one saw coming because I'm an old lady." She giggled.

When he'd been a child, she tried to keep what she did on the down low. Hunter and his siblings all knew she'd send them off to school in the morning and be home again when they returned. In between she played poker—cutthroat poker. They all knew she supported them by playing cards at various casinos in Las Vegas, but no one really talked about it. After all, she'd inherited four boisterous children when their parents had died in an automobile accident and she had to be respectable.

"I'll be there in four or maybe five hours," he said, unable to stop himself from talking. He just had to know how she had the nerve to bet her life savings for a shot at winning a casino.

"See you soon. I'll be at the *Casa de Mariposa*. It's easy to find." She disconnected.

Hunter set his phone down on the nightstand, his head spinning. What had his grandmother gotten into now? The first thing he did was call the airport, but since he couldn't get a flight until morning, he might as well drive. The arrival time would be the same. Next, he called his two brothers and sister to put them on standby. After a quick shower, he packed for a week and walked out the door of his South Beach apartment while sending text messages to his personal assistant to reschedule his appointments. Later he would let her know how far ahead she needed to reschedule.

He opened the door to the underground garage and walked to his Mercedes. A few moments later he pulled out into the thick, foggy morning air of San Francisco and headed toward the freeway.

Hunter couldn't believe his eyes. He stood in the parking lot, staring up at the elegant stately hotel that rose twelve stories up. Morning sun had already chased the desert night chill away, replacing it with rising heat. A temperature gauge on a bank across the street flashed an eighty-eight in between showing the time.

"What do you think?" Miss E. stood next to him on the sidewalk as he studied the rows of balconies that studded the side of the hotel with his inner architect eye.

The Spanish architecture was beautifully done. Painted in a glowing golden pink, the stucco façade was fancifully decorated with brightly colored mosaic trim around the doors and window, with elaborate gothic arches over the entrance to the hotel. The architectural style was a bit of a mishmash of Spanish Colonial, Moorish influence and a touch of Gothic, yet it was still pleasantly attractive and easy on the eyes.

Though he was in awe, he couldn't stop himself from scolding his grandmother. Actually, he wanted to shake her, but he was afraid she'd hurt him, so he let that notion go. "What were you thinking? Gambling your entire life savings away on a chance, a small, miniscule chance of winning a casino?" Hunter asked.

Her lips turned down in that disapproving smile that had haunted his childhood, but amusement lurked in her eyes. "I told you retirement just isn't for me. I've never been so bored in my whole life."

He leaned back on his heels, studying the façade. The hotel was on his left and the casino, contained in a three-story building, was to his right. The parking lot flanked the structure and wound around the sides. "What do you want me to do with it?" Other than some cosmetic needs, the structure looked good, though he would know better after a look at the blueprints and a more careful, detailed inspection.

Miss E. grabbed him by the front of his shirt and pulled him down to her eye level. "You don't need to do anything with this part. What I want you to do is design and oversee the building of a spa. Hot springs on the rear of the property are just going to waste. Jasper Biggins, he's the original owner, planned to build a spa, but never quite got around to it. I need you to do it."

The front doors opened at their approach and a blast of cold air flooded over them. Hunter glanced around the reception area with a knowledgeable eye.

"You need some work done in here, too." Though he had to admit the hotel was in pretty good shape. He guessed it had been built in the mid-seventies. "Just a little touch-up, a good cleaning and some professional restoration work. That's just my first impression. I have to see blueprints, do a thorough inspection, but I can find you someone good who can do that."

"I don't want someone good." Miss E. shook her head. "I want you."

They walked through the reception area after a quick

glance at the casino and out the back to the pool sparkling in the morning sun. The pool was roughly L-shaped.
Lounge chairs bordered the edges. A small cabana showed
stacks of white towels. Already half the chairs were filled
with lounging customers smearing tanning lotion on their
skin. Children played in the shallow end.

The hotel curved to his right around the pool and the
casino curved to the left. Beyond that, he saw nothing but
desert rising into hills.

His gaze traveled up over the balconies jutting out over
the pool. A couple kids stood on one, looking down. If his
brother Donovan had been there, he would have already
calculated the distance from the balcony to the pool and
considered trying a swan dive. Donovan had always been
the daredevil. Hard to believe he was now a chef in Paris.
His brother Scott had always been Donovan's co-conspir-
ator, leaving Hunter to partner with their only sister, Kenzie. If only Kenzie were here. She'd always been able to
handle Miss E., unlike Hunter and his brothers, who always seemed to be in conflict with her.

"I have a business in San Francisco." The hotel/casino
was a grand old dame, just like his grandmother.

"And you have a partner who can take up the slack. I
want you," Miss E. repeated more forcefully.

Hunter gulped. "Yes, ma'am." No one argued with Miss
E. He'd always been a tall man. Even at ten, when he first
came to live with his grandmother, he'd been taller than
her. He'd used his size to intimidate his two brothers and
sister. The one time he'd tried to intimidate his grandmother, he'd learned the hard way that no one crossed her
and lived to tell about it. He was thirty-two years old and
his grandmother could still make him feel as if he was ten.
Miss E. played poker with a lot of unsavory people and
didn't intimidate easily.

"Who's financing this?" Hunter wiped a trickle of sweat from his forehead. "You don't have that kind of money." But then again she could, and no one would ever know about it unless she wanted them to.

His grandmother waved at the top floor of the hotel. "You'll meet Miss Montgomery later. She's getting settled in one of the penthouse suites. And Reed will be along when his family emergency is taken care of."

Another thought occurred to him. Private poker games like the one his grandmother participated had a high buy-in. "How did you manage the entry fee for the game?"

"Reed and Lydia put up the buy-in money and I brought the expertise. We each own a third."

Hunter stepped back and looked up. From what he could see the structure, the bones seemed solid, though he'd know more when he started crawling around inside. They walked back into the reception area.

"This place looks frozen in time." Hunter watched a middle-aged couple step through the front doors and out into the dry July heat.

The interior was dark, heavy with wood furniture despite the most beautiful mosaic floor he'd ever seen. The long check-in counter was painted a dull brown and a woman standing behind it wore a dark brown business suit with the logo of the hotel embroidered on the pocket of her blazer. She glanced up and smiled at Miss E., then went back to whatever task she'd been doing.

The check-in area opened onto a large airy courtyard, with a pond that meandered toward the casino. The pond was a nice touch. About six feet wide and made to look like a stream, the pond bisected the approach to the casino. Small footbridges crossed over it. On one bridge a young woman stood looking down. A flash of fish caught his eye and he bent over the edge of the pond to see koi the size of his foot.

Women dressed in short flamenco skirts and ruffled blouses along with men dressed as matadors wandered the casino floor with trays, balanced on their hands, filled with various sized drinks.

The casino was really old school with slot machines that chimed out the winners along with the dings of coins into the collection bowls. The more modern casinos switched everything to digital, which were quieter and took prepaid cards instead of money.

"The hotel has four hundred twelve rooms," Miss E. said as they walked through the check-in area. "There are two restaurants, one café and a lounge. There's a small stage in the lounge for live entertainment, a couple of novelty shops at the other end of the casino and a small amphitheater for the big name acts."

Hunter sighed. "Where does the spa fit in?"

"Behind the pool is the hot springs. To take advantage of the hot springs, I think the spa needs to go there."

He would have to take a look at the area. Miss E. led him toward the bar at the edge of the casino area.

"Good morning, Miss E.," the bartender called cheerfully.

Miss E. waved at him, a happy smile on her face. "That's Roy. He's been here for years and knows where all the bodies are buried."

Hunter shook his head, still trying to process the fact his grandmother owned a casino. He wondered if his grandmother had gone insane to risk everything she had for this. "One question."

"Only one?"

He had about a million, but they'd have to wait. "What do you know about running a hotel and casino?"

She shrugged her elegant shoulders. "I know how to play poker."

So did he, because she'd taught him to play the game. "That does not make for experience in hotel management."

"I have Jasper," she said.

As if that gave him any reassurance that this wasn't a still a crazy idea. "And he is?"

"He's the previous owner and I've hired him to stay on as a consultant. I know what you're thinking, Hunter."

"No, you don't." Hunter hated when she told him exactly what he was thinking. Why couldn't she have been a bank clerk? Bank clerks didn't need to read people.

"You're wondering if I've lost my mind."

Damn, he thought. "Okay, you do know what I'm thinking. Have you lost your mind?"

She punched him on the arm. "Stop thinking that."

"What am I supposed to think?"

"That this is an incredible opportunity too good to pass up" she replied tartly.

"An incredible opportunity for what?" Poverty, starvation or homelessness?

"To be a financially independent woman, a chance to call the shots," she said.

"I'm already financially independent, and if you're worried about money, I'll take care of you."

"I don't want nor do I need you taking care of me. I can take of myself," she said, a glimmer of anger in the set line of her mouth. "I've been doing it for a few years now."

"Then why did I need to rush over here?" Hunter ran a hand over his face. He never did win an argument with her.

"Because I want my grandchildren to be a part of this."

A restaurant opened off the casino and Hunter glanced inside. "So what do you want me to do to be a part of this?"

Hunter asked. Maybe what he needed to do was to treat her like a client instead of his grandmother.

"Old world elegance brought into the twenty-first century."

"It could use a bit of toning down but without losing the elegance or class."

"Lydia will handle that." She patted him on the hand. "I just need you to come up with ideas for the spa that compliments what we're going to do on the inside."

They passed through the casino, back into the lobby and to a bank of elevators. The stream-like pond stopped thirty feet from the elevators and Hunter was surprised to see two white swans floating majestically on the water. The former owner had really understood how to create a mood. Who didn't like swans? He could have a lot of fun playing here.

An elevator opened and Miss E. led the way inside, where they were lifted steadily upward, albeit a bit slow. The inside of the elevator was more functional than elegant. Boring, Hunter thought. Whoever the previous designer had been hadn't considered how the elevators should look.

The elevator stopped on the top floor and the doors slid smoothly open. Miss E. stepped out and led the way down the hall. Only six doors opened to the hall, three on either side. They had reached the penthouse floor.

"The previous owner lived in the hotel," Miss E. explained as she stopped in front of one of the doors. "This floor has what he said were family suites." She knocked on the nearest door.

When the door opened, Hunter nearly fell to his knees. One of the most beautiful women he'd ever seen smiled at him. She was slim with a fragile, almost ethereal air to her in a Zoe Saldana way with a heart-shaped face and wide brown eyes. Shoulder-length black hair hung in long silky waves about her shoulders. Skin the color of his favorite mocha coffee looked as smooth as satin. A cream-and-black dress skimmed her body. He could tell the dress was a designer label and probably tailored to fit her. Her hands were long and slender, the nails lacquered a pale, iridescent pink to match the barely there lipstick on her pouty lips. She was so tiny a strong wind would probably blow her away. She certainly took his breath away. The longer he stood mute, the more strained her smile became until it began to falter. He was probably creeping her out.

"Oh, for heaven's sake." Miss E. pushed him into the tiled entry. "Close your mouth, Hunter. Hunter, this is Lydia. And this is Maya."

A young girl, maybe eight or nine, ran across the tiled floor and flung her arms around Miss E. Maya's resemblance to Lydia told Hunter the child was her daughter. She wore a yellow flowered sundress that showed off her light brown skin. Her long hair was woven into two thick braids that bounced against her shoulders as she ran. Instead of dark brown eyes like her mother, Maya's eyes were light amber.

"Miss Eleanor," Maya cried. "My bedroom looks like a castle. It has a princess and a prince. The prince even has a horse. I've always wanted a horse." She sighed longingly.

She grinned so wide Hunter could see new teeth coming in at the sides of her mouth. From the slight crookedness of her front teeth, braces were in her future. Yet her smile was infectious and Hunter found his own smile growing at her elfin enthusiasm.

"Lydia," Miss E. said, "this is my grandson Hunter Russell."

Lydia held out her hand. "How do you do? It's a pleasure to finally meet you." Her voice held a faint South-ern accent.

Hunter was dazed as he took her hand in his. Her skin was warm and soft. "Hello." Was that the best he could do?

"This is my daughter, Maya," Lydia said with a soft smile as she eased her hand out of his.

Maya smiled. "Hello, Mr. Russell, it's a pleasure to meet you." She held out a tiny hand for him to shake.

He solemnly accepted Maya's hand, shaking it slightly. Hunter was impressed she had manners. Like her mother. "How do you do?"

"Well, thank you." Maya giggled. For all her mannered politeness, she was still a child.

The suite was divided into three parts. The area upon walking in contained the living room. Closer to the balcony was a dining table that looked large enough to seat eight people. Beyond the sliding glass doors, he saw a pond and wondered if it had koi. On his left an open door showed a bedroom that seemed to have a child motif. Nearest the balcony was a large, open kitchen. On the other side of the living area was another open door showing a second bed-room. Across from the kitchen was another closed door, which he assumed was probably a third bedroom, and a second open door showed a white tiled bathroom.

The suite was nicely decorated with rustic red floor tiles, beige furniture and just a hint of Spanish influence in a massive sideboard holding brightly colored pottery.

"May I offer you some coffee, ice water, sweet tea?" Lydia asked in a polite voice.

"No, thank you." Hunter was still a bit shocked at his grandmother's decision to take on hotel/casino manage-ment, but even more so by the graceful, charming woman who was her business partner. She was a living piece of art.

His grandmother, on the other hand, was supposed to be

retired, to let Hunter and his siblings start taking care of her. Running a casino wasn't for the faint-hearted. Hunter didn't have a clue how to run one. Miss E. probably had an idea, but she was seventy-eight years old and was more capable of playing the game than running it.

"Come see my room, Miss E." Maya grabbed her by the hand and tugged her across the living room and into a bedroom.

He turned back to Lydia. She was watching him as closely as he had studied her. Her steady gaze unnerved him.

"I know what you're thinking." She sat down on the sofa and crossed her elegant legs, one foot bobbing up and down.

"And that is?" he asked cautiously.

"You're thinking I'm insane, we're all insane." Her voice was calm and serene.

He wasn't going to say anything negative. "Actually, I was thinking my grandmother is insane."

Lydia Montgomery was as close to perfection as a woman could be. He wondered how she could have fallen in with Miss E.

Lydia leaned forward earnestly. "Miss E. knows exactly what she's doing. And I am doing what I want to do for the first time in my life, and no one is going to stop me." A challenge lurked in her dark eyes.

Okay, she was ready for a fight. He wondered what her life had been like that she was so passionate about doing something different. "What makes you think I intend to stop my grandmother, or you?" Part of him wanted to give her whatever she wanted. He sat down in a chair that looked comfortable, but wasn't.

"I saw the way you looked at your grandmother. You looked at me the same way."

Hunter held up a hand. "I'll admit my grandmother

is pretty impulsive and I do question her sanity at times, but she is an adult. And she has all her faculties." He assumed she did. "But you…." How did he say the words struggling to get out? She looked like she belonged in a country club, not a casino.

"You think I'm going to take advantage of her, don't you?"

"I'm more concerned about my grandmother taking advantage of you."

A surprised look crossed her face as if she had to think about it for a minute. "Why would you think that?"

"Because she's a bulldozer." And Lydia looked like a stiff breeze would blow her over. "She's an expert at reading people in order to give them what they want so she can get what she wants from them."

"Your grandmother has been nothing but kind and encouraging to me. Maya adores her."

"That's how my grandma operates." Hunter remembered when he'd been under his grandmother's spell. He always fought it, but in the end gave in because giving in was so much easier. She just knew how to reel a person in like a big dumb trout.

"But…" Lydia floundered for a reply. "But she has such a clear vision. And she knows so much."

"I'm pretty sure hotel and casino management isn't on her résumé." He could hear his grandmother's voice coming from the open door of Maya's bedroom. She was laughing.

"Isn't it the same as managing a home?"

He studied her for a moment, stilled by the intensity in her chocolate brown eyes. She wasn't as frail as she looked. The way she titled her head and watched him in such a composed manner made him wonder how his grandmother had talked her into joining the poker game. "Home management and hotel management probably have similarities, but on a much larger scale."

"I'm sure Jasper is going to help us. And we do have experienced managers. And now we have you. Your grandmother thinks you're capable of rising to any occasion."

That was because his grandmother wanted him to do something. He hated feeling so cynical about Miss E. She was a master manipulator and no one got in her way when she was focused on a goal. "I have to think about this."

Her eyebrows rose. "Think fast. We have things that need to be done and you have the expertise we need." Her voice was soft and almost commanding. Something about her reminded him a bit of Miss E. She wasn't asking him, but commanding him to do her bidding. Maybe he should get back in his car and return to San Francisco. His grandmother was a force of nature, but this woman looked soft and yielding yet already he could see she had a will of iron. She reminded him a little bit of a pit bull.

He forced himself not to smile or give in to make her happy. This woman was lethal. "What do you think I can do?"

"This is a luxury hotel and casino, and while we need to maintain our older clients, we also need to find a way to attract a younger clientele. Older clients think luxury comes with the room, but younger clients are willing to pay extra for them. And the one thing I've noticed after a couple months here in Reno and in Lake Tahoe is that there is money here. It's quiet money, not very flashy, and buried deep. And I want to get that money for this hotel."

He was surprised about her assumption about Reno. She had a depth to her that her exterior only hinted at. And any man would be a fool to underestimate her. "And you want a spa. Classy, elegant and…"

"Restful. A spa should be a treat. People want to be pampered."

Me, too, Hunter thought. "Who doesn't want to be pampered?"

"I want to create a more understated elegance. I want class with that comfort." She closed her eyes while she thought, leaning back against the colorful cushions.

You want you. Maybe Miss E. wasn't wrong about bringing Lydia Montgomery in. She knew what women wanted. "Understated elegance and comfort costs money. How far are you willing to go to get that?"

"I have money. Not as much as Reed Watson, but enough to cover my third ownership."

"Who is this Reed person?"

She opened her eyes. "I haven't met him since he's away dealing with a family emergency. I do understand he's a good friend to your grandmother."

Hunter needed to check up on Reed Watson. "What do you consider elegant?"

She tilted her head, thinking. "Renaissance, Italy. Beautiful gowns, beautiful furniture. Elizabethan England. Regency England. Or maybe art deco, art nouveau. Or maybe Paris in the thirties. Josephine Baker, Langston Hughes, James Baldwin. Imperial Japan was beautiful. I can just see serene gardens and koi ponds like the one in the lobby." Her eyes went dreamy and far away as she recited her litany of possibilities. "Napoleonic France." Her face glowed with her ideas.

"These times of incredible beauty were always precursors to incredible disasters and upheavals," Hunter said. Her enthusiasm was contagious. He just wanted to impress her. Who the hell didn't want to do that for her?

She opened her eyes and glared at him, her dark eyes shining. "Mr. Russell, I am impressed that you know your history, but you're ruining my dreams with your knowledge."

"Hunter. Please call me Hunter. I'm an architect and being practical goes with my job description." He understood the importance of artistic aesthetics, but they warred with functionality every time. His specialty was the preservation of historic homes. He'd never built a spa before. If he accepted the challenge, he would be spending time with Lydia, getting to know her. He turned over all the possibilities in his mind.

"You smell a challenge," she said.

"I'm not sure I like that smug look on your face."

"You're in. I can tell."

"I'm thinking." Hunter didn't like knowing how easily anyone—especially Lydia—could read him. "Why are you doing this?" Thoughts whirled around in his brain and the idea of a spa started to appeal to him. He would have to do some research, but research was something that came naturally to him.

She was silent for so long he thought she wasn't going to answer him. Finally, she said, "I don't want my daughter to grow up like me."

She surprised him with her honesty. He definitely wanted to know more. What had happened in her childhood to make her want something so different for her daughter? She was an interesting mix of sophistication and naiveté. "What's wrong with you?"

She took a deep breath. "I was raised to be a…a decoration—first for my parents and then my late husband. If my daughter sees me doing something of value then she will know there is more to life than hosting cocktail parties and rearranging flowers."

Hunter could think of nothing to say after that statement. He had a feeling not one ounce of fun had been built into her youth.

Maya came running back into the living room. Miss E. followed at a more sedate pace. "Momma, Miss E. and I were talking about horses. She thinks I should have one."

Lydia gave Miss E. a long, thoughtful look. "She does, does she?"

Maya nodded enthusiastically, hands clasped in front of her, eyes pleading. "Can I have a horse, please, so I can ride with my prince?"

Hunter forced himself not to smile. Miss E. was at it again. His grandmother was the pied piper.

"Every young girl should know how to control a huge beast like a horse so she can learn how to control the two-legged kind."

Hunter gave his grandmother a sharp look. "Is that how you learned?"

"My daddy raised bird dogs and I grew up with horses so I learned at a young age about horses and dogs and later on, children."

"You raised us like we were puppies?"

"And look how you turned out. I should write a book." Miss E.'s eyes sparkled with amusement. "Raising your children to bark on command."

Lydia burst out laughing. "At one time I wanted to take horseback riding lessons myself."

"Why didn't you?"

She sighed. "My parents didn't consider it an acceptable sport for a proper young lady."

Now that was sad. His parents and later his grandmother indulged all of them in their interests. He was beginning to dislike Lydia's parents. "What are you going to tell her?" He gestured at Maya.

Lydia hugged her daughter. "I'll consider it."

Miss E. leaned over Hunter and whispered, "She's in."

As if Hunter didn't already know that. Frankly, so was he. He was just going to make them work a bit harder for it.

Maya leaned against her mother's knee, her eyes pleading. "Please, please, please."

"I said I'd consider it. Horses bite." Lydia brushed a few flyaway tendrils of her daughter's dark hair away from her face.

"We'll find one that doesn't bite," Miss E. said, a note of finality in her tone.

Oh, yeah, Maya was getting a horse. And he was getting a new job…at least for a while. He would have to call his partner and arrange for him to take over his clients. He needed to call his assistant and let her know. A list formed in his mind. The logistics of what he was about to do made him wonder if he was the one who was insane.

Lydia didn't realize how bored she'd been with her life until she met Miss E. Miss E. lived a life Lydia could only dream about. She'd lived on her luck and her wits while raising her grandchildren. She'd taken risks, never knowing if she would win or lose, while shaping her own destiny. If Lydia didn't know any better, she might have been jealous. Lydia wasn't very comfortable knowing that about herself. Jealousy was bad. Jealousy was a sin. She had heard that often enough from the pulpit of the Baptist church her parents attended.

Lydia grinned at her daughter flying through the suite, putting her clothes away. Lydia had wanted a pony, too, but her parents had enrolled her in ballet in order to learn to be graceful and fluid. Yes, she had learned gracefulness, but also how to appreciate music and be resilient, how to balance and develop her eye-hand coordination.

She had loved ballet as a child, but she'd really wanted a horse, just like Maya.

"Your son is very forceful," Lydia said to Miss E. after Hunter left. And handsome. She was glad he was gone because he made her feel…she wasn't sure what. But whatever it was left her uncomfortable because for a brief second her gaze had settled on his lips and she'd wondered what it would be like to be kissed by him. Miss E. laughed. "He's the oldest and thinks he's expected to act in such a manner. Underneath he's a pussycat." Miss E. paused in the act of zipping up a suitcase. "You're not going to let him scare you because he thinks I'm eccentric, are you?"

"I don't think I've ever met anyone who has all their marbles like you do." Everybody who had sat down at that poker table had been at least thirty years younger than Miss E., and she'd outwitted them all. "You are living, breathing proof that experience is the most valuable asset."

"An asset you need to develop."

"I'm nothing compared to you," Lydia said almost ashamedly.

"You have skills I will never have. I sat down at the table with a bunch of men who knew my reputation and knew not to underestimate me, but you, with your beautiful face, charming manner and soft voice—no one looks at you and thinks that underneath you have a will of steel."

"I don't have that," Lydia objected, thinking of all the times she'd obediently followed her mother's orders just to be nice.

"You underestimate yourself. The second the door on your gilded cage was unlocked, you flew away."

"I had no plan." Running away from New Orleans had been impulsive and possibly silly. She'd done so anyway because she couldn't stand the feeling of being cloistered, of being locked up.

"Yes, you did. You snatched your daughter and fled. You waited until you found someone…me…who would help you. You didn't just walk into my poker school to learn to play poker for fun. You needed a skill. You needed to learn how to outwit people with what you think you don't have."

Lydia stared in astonishment at Miss E. If anything else, learning to play poker had taught her to keep her cards close to her vest and learn strategy. "How did you know that about me? I didn't even know that about me."

"I watched you watching people. In the three months you've been here, you've become a better poker player than ninety percent of the people I've ever taught. That's because they were playing for fun and you weren't. They wanted to win money and you wanted to win respect. I know you like it when people underestimate you."

Lydia stared into the older woman's shrewd eyes, frowning. "I'm not that good at poker."

Miss E. simply smiled. "You don't play cards, you play the cards, you play the people. You manipulate them by your actions. Do you know how many tournaments I've won and never even looked at my cards?"

"Miss Eleanor, you make me sound so manipulative." But wasn't she? she asked herself. How often had her husband brought home some little piece of jewelry because she admired it and had manipulated him into purchasing it? Once he bought her a brand new Lexus because she'd complained about the Cadillac. And she'd managed to keep Maya out of the prestigious boarding school Mitchell thought would be good for her by batting her eyes and telling him how much Maya was an asset for his business. All because he made profitable contacts through Maya's friends in the fancy private school she attended. She didn't care about his business as much as she wanted to keep

Maya home with her. She had used Mitchell's ego to get what she'd wanted. He'd given in because he adored Maya and deep down inside wanted to keep her home, too.

"You're a beautiful, fragile woman and your ability to manipulate is your greatest weapon. You keep letting people underestimate you, because when you knock them on their butt, they are still not going to get it. And mark my words, you're going to knock Hunter on his butt and I'm going to enjoy watching you."

Lydia sat down on the sofa and let her thoughts wander. "Thinking back, I believe you might be right." Unfortunately her actions reminded her of her mother and made her uncomfortable. Caroline Fairchild had gotten what she wanted the very same way Lydia had. Lydia wanted to change that part of herself.

"You fascinate me, my dear. I read you five minutes after we met." Miss E. opened the closet door and hung up Maya's dresses. Maya had retreated to a corner of the bedroom with her dolls, and sat on the floor playing quietly.

Lydia ran over in her mind why she'd come to Reno when she could have gone anywhere. She had more money than she could spend in a thousand lifetimes. She had global contacts and time.

Maybe Hunter had figured her out. Reno was as different as she could get. No one would think to look for her here. At least not for a while. And from the frantic phone messages left by her two stepsons, they were definitely looking for her. She kept her phone turned off most of the time because she didn't want David and Leon to find her anytime soon. Eventually, they'd hire someone to track her down. And she would be ready for them, digging in her heels and making a life for herself in Reno despite any objections they would have.

She heard Miss E. laughing with Maya, which turned

Lydia's thoughts to Hunter Russell. He was a handsome man with his lean face and muscular body. His brown eyes had been as shrewd and sharp as his grandmother's. Yet, he made her uncomfortable. Unlike Mitchell, who had been thirty-five years older than her. Mitchell had been a quiet, almost comfortable man. He'd asked little of her except to look pretty on his arm, to be gracious to his friends and to make his life comfortable. She had rather liked Mitchell even though he'd been her parents' choice and not hers. Her marriage had not been the exciting relationship she had dreamed of, but it had been fruitful. Mitchell had given her Maya and for that she would always be thankful.

He'd asked Lydia if he could name the child after his mother and she'd agreed because she thought the name was so beautiful. She always suspected he'd been more of father to Maya than to his other two children.

She'd done everything Mitchell asked despite her dislike of his two grown sons from his first marriage. Leon and David Montgomery had hated her from the moment they'd met her. She'd been twenty-one and barely out of college when she'd married Mitchell. Leon and David had been in their early thirties. Leon was the consummate playboy, with two illegitimate children whose mothers had to sue him for child support, while David married every stripper he'd ever met. Crippled beneath the mountain of alimony David had to pay out every month, Lydia had the idea he'd been almost delighted when Mitchell had died until the will had been read and he'd discovered Maya had inherited most of the money and the businesses, with Lydia as the executer.

"I think we're mostly done with the unpacking," Miss E. said a moment later. She closed the last suitcase and zipped it. "I'll just call the front desk and have them send someone up to collect the luggage and put it in storage."

"Thank you." Lydia nodded absently. "What about you? Have you decided on which suite you're going to use?"

"I'm staying in my RV for the time being," Miss E. answered. "I've lived in that RV for ten years. I'm not quite ready to give it up." Her RV was parked in a side lot and plugged into the hotel's electric grid. Lydia had never been in an RV before until she'd met Miss E. and she had found it to be quite comfortable if a bit cramped. She'd even considered buying her own, learning to drive it and then taking Maya all over the country to see all the wonderful places Lydia had always wanted to see. "So what happens next?"

Miss E. and Lydia went into the living room to sit down in chairs that faced each other, leaving Maya to play in her bedroom.

Miss E.'s face was thoughtful. "Reed and I have discussed letting you take over building the spa with Hunter while we take over the casino upgrades. Jasper is going to act as our consultant."

"Do you know when Reed will be coming?"

"I don't know. He said his father is doing better, but he's going to be in the hospital for a couple more weeks and his mother isn't handling it well," Miss E. said.

"How does a computer geek decide he wants to own a casino?" Lydia wondered. Reed Watson had been a computer nerd of the highest degree, starting his social media company in his bedroom while still in high school and then selling it ten years later for 2.9 billion dollars.

Miss E. shrugged. "It was on his bucket list. He has the most extensive bucket list for such a young man who's barely thirty."

Lydia laughed. "I hate to say anything bad, but I hope he doesn't kick the bucket before we're done."

Miss E. laughed with her. After she left, Lydia found a pad of paper in the desk in her bedroom and sat down to put together her list of ideas for the spa.

Chapter 2

Hunter appropriated an empty office and tried not to look at the velvet paintings hanging on the wall. One was of dogs playing poker. Another was of Elvis. And the third was of a deer with a target drawn around it. Hunter couldn't identify the significance of any of the paintings—except for the one of the dogs. He sort of liked the one of a young Elvis, microphone in hand, hips gyrating. He left it hanging, and took the others down, stacking them in a corner facing the wall.

The desk was a little rickety, but a matchbook under one leg steadied it. Across the scarred wooden top, he'd spread out the original blueprints for the hotel. *Casa de Mariposa* had been built in the late seventies just as Reno really started to grow. The best materials had been used. At least he had something to work with and the builder hadn't used cheap materials.

A knock sounded on the door and he called the person in. Lydia opened the door and smiled at him. "Do you have a moment?"

He felt a tiny thrill at the sight of her. Since he'd met her yesterday, the image of her delicate face had hovered around the edges of his thoughts. He'd been so fixated on his career for the past ten years, he'd put love and marriage on the back burner. He dated, but avoided serious relationships. "What can I do for you?"

She stepped into the room and looked around. "Now that I've had a day to look this place over," she said, "it's… it's so…overwhelming."

Hunter grinned. "I know."

"Did you know there is a mechanical bull in the Ranchero lounge and…" Words seemed to fail her. "Apparently, Jasper liked to ride it."

"I rode one once," Hunter admitted.

Her eyes went wide. "You?"

"Not one of my prouder moments. A friend was getting married and he and his girl had their rehearsal dinner at a country western place and somehow I got shamed into trying one." He'd stayed on the mechanical bull a total of three seconds.

"Was alcohol involved?"

"Do I look like the type of man who would get on a mechanical bull clear-headed?"

She tilted her head, squinting her eyes. "You look like the type of man who should be able to hold his liquor and act sensibly."

His grin widened. "That was a nice way to say I was an idiot."

"I pride myself on my tact."

He laughed and after a second's hesitation she laughed, too. She was so pretty, but had a serious look in her dark brown eyes. She needed to laugh more. She seemed so reined in, as though she always had to behave in a manner appropriate to someone else's dictates. He wondered what her husband had been like. Miss E. had given him a little background about her over dinner last night. He thought arranged marriages were a thing of the past. He wondered if she'd been happy. Whatever her husband had been like, he appeared to have taken good care or her.

"Why are you looking at me like that?" she asked looking nervous.

"You must have an interesting story."

"Hardly." Her tone was dry and slightly sarcastic, letting him know her background was off limits.

"You underestimate yourself." Today she wore a flowered yellow and blue silk blouse and dark blue silk pants and matching blue shoes with little heels. She'd knotted a yellow scarf about her neck. A gold pendant showed in the hollow of her throat.

Hunter felt underdressed in jeans and a knit pullover. One knee had a frayed hole just starting and the pullover had a small smear of dirt on it from his rummaging around a storage room looking for the blueprints. He could have gotten them at the building department, but that would have taken time.

"I thought we could take a look at the area around the hot springs and think about the spa," she said.

"Did you see this place before Miss E. won it?"

"Yes, the poker game was held here," she replied. "I loved it from the moment I walked in. As overpowering as the hotel is in some ways, there is a real beauty here, but a lot of the heavy Spanish decor hides it. My fingers itch to start making changes."

"Why a spa?"

She looked down, her face showing uncertainty. "There are a lot of wealthy women in Tahoe, Sacramento and San Francisco who want first-rate mani-pedis and massages. They choose the places they want to visit based on the spa facilities. If we have a first-rate spa, we'll be able to attract those women."

"Then let's take a look."

* * *

The hot springs was a series of small pools that covered about an acre. Small paths meandered around and between the pools. Rocks were strewn around the ground bordering the springs. The ground sloped gently down to the water's edge. Someone had positioned benches on the paths. The area felt remote even though the hotel was a few hundred feet away.

Hunter could understand why Lydia wanted to put a spa here. The area was peaceful and serene. Civilization seemed to be so far away. Hunter shaded his eyes, expertly assessing the surrounding area and mentally starting to build the spa from the ground up. He wanted something unobtrusive that would work with the natural beauty of the land.

"I was in England a few years ago," Lydia said when they stood on the edge of the hot springs. "One of the places I went to was Bath. The Roman baths were so beautiful. I wonder if there's any way we can duplicate that kind of atmosphere here.

"I've been to Bath, too. I studied architecture in London." He looked around, gauging the possibilities. In his mind's eye, he calculated how to best work out the layout of the spa. Nothing too elaborate. He was all about keeping things simple and clean.

"You did. What a great adventure you must have had." She gave him a shy look.

"I learned a lot about historical preservation. It was incredible. To think that something people built lasted a thousand years and more without falling down was quite a departure for me. Our own culture is into tearing down and rebuilding." Usually into something ugly and irritatingly modern. That had been the real reason why he'd gone into historical preservation. The past was important and obliterating it by pulling buildings down severed an important link to who people used to be.

The challenge of creating the spa gave him a tiny thrill of excitement. Unlike Las Vegas, Reno was still doing ticky-tacky. The Mariposa was a diamond amidst the glaring lights of the tacky. This city needed more style, class and elegance. Maybe then people would stop thinking of Reno as Las Vegas's ugly baby sister.

The water sparkled in the morning sun. A large hawk spiraled lazily overhead. The tall grass rustled in the light wind. Trees dotted the area around the springs and more benches were situated under them to take advantage of the shade.

"Isn't it beautiful here?" She sat down on a bench and gazed at the water. "This would be a great place for dining."

"That's not a bad idea. You could serve lunch and keep people here all day."

"But don't you want people to spend their money at the gaming tables?" she asked.

"Of course, but if we do this spa right, it could be a big attraction and money maker. The whole point is to draw people in and make them stay here, along with their money."

The hot springs spread out over a half acre, with sloped foothills beyond gradually growing to the higher, jagged peaks of the Sierra Nevada Mountains. The sound of running water created a serenity that could make this place a refuge for tired gamblers who wanted a bit of pampering.

"When you say do this right, what do you mean?" Lydia shaded her eyes with one hand as she studied the terrain.

"I have an idea working around in the back of my head. When it germinates, I'll share it with you. It's going to take a bit of time." In the dirt he noticed what he thought were deer tracks. Identifying tracks was one thing he recalled from his time as a Boy Scout.

She clapped her hands like a child. "The creative process at work. I'm so envious."

"What makes you think you don't have any creativity?"

She shrugged.

"For all you know, you may just be the world's greatest macaroni artist. You just haven't discovered your talent yet."

She laughed lightly. "I have no desire to be a macaroni artist."

He loved her laugh. She sounded so carefree. She needed to be this way more often. "Give it a try. You may never know."

"I'll start working on my portrait of Elvis right away. I can hang it right next to your velvet painting of him."

"You can borrow the velvet painting for inspiration."

"No, thank you." Her tone was always so polite. "I couldn't believe it when I saw it."

"It kinda grows on you after a while."

Lydia knelt down and dipped her fingers in the heated water. "This feels so good. I can just see women lounging in the water, sipping glasses of cool white wine, or maybe sherry." She closed her eyes and wriggled her fingers in the water. "I want to jump in right now."

Anyone for skinny-dipping? Hunter thought. He watched her, the pure joy on her face, the way her lips curved upward so slightly in a smile that wasn't quite a smile. She did that a lot and he wondered if her mother had told her smiling too much created wrinkles. Even though he hadn't met the woman he had the feeling her mother would say exactly that.

He wanted to help her make the spa a success because he wanted her to be successful. He would do everything in his power to make the dream a reality. He wanted to be her hero. That and a few other things.

Lydia left Maya with her tutor and went to find a suitable office for herself. Louisiana schools and Nevada schools had different curriculums, and Maya needed to be brought up to speed before September, when she would attend a local Reno school. Until she'd moved to Reno, Lydia had never thought about things like differing curriculums. Reno seemed to have its own culture and that culture was so different from New Orleans. New Orleans was old money, sedate and dignified or wild and excessive. Reno was new money, brash and still a bit rough around the edges. She liked it. Reno seemed to have an energy New Orleans lacked. She wanted to be a part of that rough-and-tumble, all-American vibe Reno had. New Orleans was all about history and culture. Reno was fresh and about new beginnings. It was redefining itself from a wild west frontier town to an exciting, eclectic city that was all about growth and new business.

The casino, which had been mostly empty during the morning, grew to bustling as the afternoon progressed. Miss E. was meeting with the Gaming Commission and then her lawyer. Jasper had gone with her to help expedite the change in ownership. Getting everything changed into the names of the new owners was turning into a huge task. Owning a casino was not like owning any other businesses. Not only did the three new owners need to be investigated by the state, but by the federal government to make sure they were free of any unsavory connections. The only thing not required was a blood sample. Hunter had sequestered himself in the office he'd requisitioned as he pored over the original blueprints for the resort. Lydia felt the need to find her own office.

When she found a small, out-of-the-way room that seemed to be nothing but storage, Lydia claimed it as hers. Maintenance workers were currently emptying it and she held a tape measure in one hand and a notebook in the other as she made note of all the dimensions of the room and her thoughts on how she wanted to decorate it. Nothing too elaborate but something tasteful and elegant, a place she could be the woman she wanted to be. But the room needed to be comfortable. She would need filing cabinets, a desk and chair. She already had her laptop, but she would need internet and a hundred other things that raced around in her head. What an exciting venture she was starting on.

The maintenance supervisor nodded at her list. He would have everything she needed in a couple of hours. He even had some paint to brighten up the walls. He listed the colors he had and she asked for just plain white. He told her the office would be ready for her in the morning and she smiled her gratitude, thrilled to get started.

Her cell phone rang and she answered it.

"Mrs. Montgomery, this is the front desk," came a man's soothing, pleasant voice. "There are two men here to see you."

"I'll be right there." Who could possibly be looking for her?

She walked to the lobby and stopped suddenly. Leon and David had found her. Rubbing the corners of her eyes, she walked up to her stepsons. She'd hoped for a little more time to prepare for whatever nastiness they were planning to throw at her.

"Leon. David," she said pleasantly. "What are you doing so far away from home?"

Leon was the elder of the two and time had not treated him graciously. Frown lines marred the corners of his mouth and his eyes were hard and cold. Though his suit jacket was cut well, it didn't quite hide the slight expansion of his waist. His hands were soft and well-manicured. David was the epitome of soft, pampered and almost charming. Like his brother, he'd never really worked. Both held token jobs in their father's real estate development business, but they held no real power. Power they both craved. Power that had been denied them at the reading of the will.

Leon glared at Lydia. "Thought you could hide from us forever, didn't you."

"I didn't keep my whereabouts a secret," she said calmly. She hadn't seen fit to tell them where she was going, she didn't need to. "Any connection we have is over. You've both made it quite clear you no longer wanted to have anything to do with me."

"That didn't mean you could just disappear with our sister." Leon's voice was low and threatening.

"I believe you once referred to Maya as my ATM machine." Lydia stiffened even though she trembled inside. Standing up to these two angry men was difficult, which one of the reasons why she'd simply left. They'd never cared for her when their father was alive. Why they should care now was beyond her.

Leon scowled at her. "David and I were hoping we could put this in the past."

David stepped forward, one hand on his brother's arm. "We'd like to spend some time with Maya."

"I beg your pardon?" With one eyebrow lifted, she tilted her head at them.

"We miss her," David replied.

His singular lack of sincerity alerted her. Something was wrong, but what? David and Leon had never given Maya the time of day, much less wanted to spend time with her.

"I doubt that," she finally said, her tone dry. She wanted to be pleasant to these two men, but something in their posture made her wary. "But if you want to spend time with Maya, I'll be happy to speak to my lawyer to see what kind of visitation we can work out."

Leon pushed forward. "You don't trust us with our sister!"

Lydia studied him. She wouldn't trust him with the stuffed animals in Maya's bedroom.

"Trust has nothing to do with it. But I have to make sure that we all understand exactly where we stand on this issue. Maya's well-being is at stake here."

Leon took a deep breath. "You pulled her away from everything she knew to this…this…seedy little backwoods gambling town. I fear for her moral welfare." He tried to look outraged, but failed.

"Since when have you been worried about Maya's moral barometer? If I remember correctly, your ex-paramour had to take you to court to get you to pay child support for your two children, who you claimed weren't yours to get out of taking responsibility for them. And David, you've been married to three different Bourbon Street strippers. Such classy wives you chose."

David shrugged.

Leon looked furious. "We don't own a casino that preys on people's weaknesses."

"If I remember correctly, your father paid your gambling debts a time or three, or maybe four. Or was it five times?" Lydia hated getting nasty with these two, but being nice never seemed to work with them.

Leon scowled. "You're corrupting Maya and we don't like that."

"You don't have a say in how I raise Maya. And if you don't mind," she looked at her watch, "I have to pick up my morally fragile daughter from her tutor and take her to her amoral ballet lesson."

"Until you talk to your lawyer, David and I will be staying." A small gleam of triumph glittered in Leon's eyes.

"I'm sure Reno has enough vices to occupy you both. Enjoy your stay." Lydia turned on her heel and headed for the elevator, trying not to have a full-blown panic attack.

They were up to something. Thoughts whirled around her brain as she tried to figure out her stepsons' intentions.

Once she was in her suite, she walked into her bedroom after quickly hugging Maya and giving her instructions to get ready for her ballet lesson. She also graciously thanked the tutor for her time. She leaned against the closed door for a second and then took out her phone and called Mitchell's lawyer in New Orleans.

Everest Tynan had a warm, welcoming voice. "I was expecting your call."

"You were. Did you know David and Leon are in Reno? They're being a bit obnoxious."

"I suspected you were going to have some trouble from your two stepchildren."

"They arrived a little while ago. They appear to be concerned about Maya's moral development."

Everest snorted. And Lydia found herself almost smiling. Everest was a man of very limited emotional responses and the fact that he'd snorted told her the whole situation was ludicrous.

"They came to see me," Everest continued. "They want visitation rights with Maya."

"That is what they said, but I'm suspicious. They never wanted anything to do with Maya when Mitchell was alive."

"I agree, and since you're now a resident of Nevada, I did some research and put together a list of Reno lawyers.

I'll text them to your phone. They are all excellent lawyers. I suggest you contact one. David and Leon are there to make trouble and you need legal representation to make sure Maya's rights are taken care of."

"Thank you." Everest Tynan had always been loyal to Mitchell and on Mitchell's death had transferred that loyalty to Maya. Maya had always been able to twist him around her little finger. Lydia would always be grateful for him and the way he helped her through the torturous months after Mitchell's death. Even though Lydia had never been in love with Mitchell, she had loved him more like a father because he was so different from her own father. He had indulged her and adored Maya. Lydia would have been content the rest of her life with Mitchell. But cancer was so unpredictable. Sixty-four was too young to die, but it was not unexpected.

Lydia felt tears gather in her eyes. Suddenly, she missed him so much her heart ached with intense pain. They'd been talking about a second child when he'd been struck down. A part of her would never get over him, but in the last year, her grief had eased.

"Take care, Lydia. I'll be talking with you soon."

"You take care, too." She disconnected. If she missed anyone from New Orleans, it was Everest. And maybe her mother a little bit, too.

The coffee shop was a tiny little alcove off the main lobby. Lydia ordered a decaf latte and turned around to look for a table. She found Hunter tucked in a corner, a cup of coffee at his elbow, a half-eaten piece of apple pie and his laptop open in front of him.

The café was a pleasant place with cheerful colors, black-and-white tile on the floor, red vinyl booths and a long counter with red-covered stools. The café was very clean, right down to the corners, but small signs of wear showed in the chipped Formica on the snack counter and small cracks in the vinyl covering the booths.

"Can I join you?" Lydia asked Hunter. Even though she hated to interrupt, she just liked being around him. Even though they'd only know each other a couple days, he made her feel safe, and even more important, he made her feel special. He looked at her as though she was a person who was capable of making an intelligent decision. He treated her like a real person not a doll to be put up on a shelf and dusted every once in a while. And the way he made her heart race. Well, actually that bothered her a bit, but she liked that he made her feel alive.

Hunter looked up and smiled. He closed his laptop. "I hear we have new guests in the hotel."

She took a long sip of her coffee, trying to calm her nerves. "Yes, my stepsons. It's family reunion time."

He smiled. "I can see you're overjoyed."

"Just get it out of your system," she said, liking the way his eyes crinkled at the corners like a real smile.

"What do you mean?"

"Your opinions about my stepchildren being older than me."

"Commenting on such a thing would be…crude."

"The fact that you know my stepsons are older than me, and they've only been in the hotel less than an hour, tells me people are gossiping already. So just get it over with."

"I'm sure it's awkward, having them underfoot."

"It's more awkward not knowing what they want." She tapped her fingers on the table.

"Maybe they just want to spend time with you." He looked as though he didn't believe his words, but they had to be said.

Her eyes narrowed, and held her fingers over her mouth

to prevent the building torrent of words from coming forth. That would be unladylike and rude. "I'm sure they have a reason to be here, but I can guarantee you it's not to be sociable with me."

He held up a finger. "Give me a second while I find the right response."

He thought and finally said, "Okay, I don't have the right response."

"I don't either, but I do know I don't want them here."

He shrugged his broad shoulders. "You're part owner of the place. Call security and have them remove your step-kiddies."

She thought about that for a second. As much as that idea appealed to her, it would simply make things worse, or worse than they already were.

He leaned forward, his amber-colored eyes intense. "You look like you're plotting."

"I am." Though for a second she was distracted by his closeness. Her gaze lingered on his lips. They were full and seductive. She had so little experience with men and yet she couldn't stop from thinking what it would feel like to be kissed by him.

"Need any help?" Hunter looked eager.

She laughed, happy to have a partner in crime. One she suspected she could trust implicitly. Lydia liked that. "I'm wondering what I can do to make Leon's and David's stay here as unpleasant as possible without jeopardizing the reputation of this hotel."

"Therein is the rub."

She shuddered to think what Leon and David wanted. "They've already angered the housekeeping staff." Having those two in her hotel was going to be a huge problem. "And they haven't even unpacked yet."

"How is it that Maya is so well-behaved and these two crybabies seem like they're entitled snobs?"

A sense of pride engulfed her. Hunter was telling her she was a good mother. Did he have any idea how important that was to her? "Because their mother raised them to be entitled snobs, in my opinion. And while Maya is no wilting flower, she is allowed to speak her mind, as long as she is respectful." She rested her elbow on the table and cupped her chin in her palm. Miss Eleanor would never take such treatment from them. She wasn't going to either. "I believe I will let the staff know they are under no obligation to go above and beyond their normal duties on my stepsons' behalf."

"You do have some claws," he said, admiration in his tone.

Surprised, she studied him, her head tilted. "I'm tired of people walking all over me. I had to put up with them while married to their father, but I no longer have to do that." She felt proud of herself. She thought of how many times she'd retreated from confrontation for the sake of family harmony and she wasn't going to do so anymore. She liked this feeling of empowerment. Now if she could just carry through with it without asking Hunter for help. But then she thought, no. She could do this on her own, although she was glad to have such a strong ally at her side. She had to learn to handle unpleasant situations by herself. She had known her position would not be easy, but Mitchell had deflected so much of his sons' rancor from her.

She took another sip of her coffee while her thoughts churned. Hunter had finished his slice of apple pie. Her phone rang and she glanced at the display. David. Should she answer it? She decided she might as well.

"Hello, David."

"Hello, Lydia," he said jovially. "Dinner at eight in the little restaurant with the matador theme."

"I'm sorry, what did you say?"

"Dinner at eight."

"I don't think so."

A long silence stretched out between them. Finally, he said, "Please."

That caught her off guard. David and Leon never said please for anything. It was always a demanding "Give me this" or "Give me that."

"No," she said. She had dinner planned with Maya and Miss Eleanor. "I have a business dinner." Though business wouldn't be the primary focus of the meal, she was certain business would be discussed at some point.

She heard David suck in his breath. "This is important, Lydia." His voice had gone hard. "It concerns Maya."

She took a breath and held it for a second before letting it out slowly. She would not knuckle under to their demands. "I'll meet you for drinks at nine o'clock in the lounge."

A sigh of exasperation came through the phone. "Fine," he said sharply. David disconnected without another word.

"Do you know where Miss E. is?" she asked Hunter.

"She was in the casino talking to one of the pit bosses."

Lydia pushed herself to her feet and glanced at her watch. She had twenty minutes before she had to leave to pick up Maya from her ballet lesson. "I need to talk to her." And she walked away, realizing she'd just been rude to Hunter. She walked back and smiled at him. "Thank you." And turned once again and left the café.

Lydia found Miss E. standing in the entryway to the casino. Slot machines dinged cheerfully, waitresses in skimpy flamenco outfits wandered among the patrons pushing drinks. Miss E. had a wide smile on her face.

"Isn't this wonderful." Miss E. spread her hands to indicate that most of the machines had people seated in front of them feeding their change into the hungry slots. A slot machine dinged and someone shouted in delight. Another winner.

"This place is overpowering," Lydia said. "Where are you starting?"

"Like I said, one room at a time, dear. We will make this the most exciting place the Reno. I talked to my grand-daughter, Kenzie, and she has a friend who does some sort of public relations voodoo. I wanted to talk to you and Reed about hiring her to help us change our image. We need to sex it up."

"I beg your pardon? You mean skimpy flamenco outfits aren't sexy enough?"

Miss E. grinned. "I don't mean the staff. I'm talking about the casino and the hotel."

"That sounds like a start, but right now I need some help." She held out her phone with the text from Everest. "It seems Mitchell's children have arrived to make my life unbearable."

"I heard," Miss E. said with a sigh, "from the wait staff, from room service, from housekeeping, the concierge and the bell hops."

Lydia massaged her temples. "I don't know what they want, but I have a feeling I'm going to need a lawyer. Do you know any of these names my lawyer in Louisiana sent me?" She held up her phone and showed the email message to Miss E.

Miss E. took the phone and scrolled down the list, a faint frown putting a crease in her forehead. She stopped scrolling. "Vanessa Peabody. Good poker player. Try her first. Any idea at all on what they want?"

"They told me they want visitation rights with Maya. But I suspect they have something else in mind. David and Leon have always been the type to say one thing and do another." Lydia pocketed the phone. The feeling she was going to find out over drinks just exactly what Leon and David wanted filled her with dread. "They're going to cause trouble." Trouble followed them wherever they went.

"Then you'd best be talking to Vanessa right now." She pulled her own cell phone out of her pants pocket.

"You have her on speed dial!"

"A good doctor, a good accountant and a good lawyer is how you keep a well-balanced and happy life." Miss E. spoke into the phone and five minutes later Lydia had an appointment with Vanessa Peabody.

"I've been trying to take care of things by myself."

"You are taking care of things. You came to me for advice." Miss E. patted her cheek. "Good hunting, dear."

The lounge was dark and quiet. At the grand piano sat a man playing soothing music. The muted ding of the slot machines from the casino drifted in. Lydia arrived early and ordered a soda. Vanessa Peabody sat at the table immediately adjoining Lydia's.

"Now," Vanessa said quietly, "listen to what they have to say. I'll be taking notes. Don't tell them I'm here or they might get antagonistic."

Lydia nodded, her throat too choked for her to say anything.

"And relax," Vanessa murmured as she sipped her soda.

Lydia concentrated on her breathing as she waited, trying to maintain an exterior calm when her insides trembled so hard she thought the table would shake.

A shadow fell over her and she glanced up. David slid into the booth across from her and Leon followed. Both men stared at her. David looked slightly petulant while Leon's cold eyes appraised Lydia.

"Good evening," she said as politely as she could manage even though her throat was so tight she could barely speak.

"Let's dispense with the pleasantries," Leon replied. A waitress approached and both men ordered bourbon. David's was over ice; Leon preferred his neat.

"Of course," Lydia said, expecting exactly that.

David shrugged while Leon looked astonished at her being agreeable.

"David and I have decided that it would be in Maya's best interest if one of us had custody of her."

Shocked, Lydia could only stare. *Take a breath before you speak,* she heard Vanessa's voice in the back of her head. She took several deep breaths, trying to calm herself down before she said anything.

"Why would you think that?" She put her hands in her lap so they wouldn't see her shaking.

"Look at this place," Leon said, disgust clearly on his face. "You can't raise a sensitive child, like Maya, in a casino. This place is tawdry, pedestrian and vulgar. She needs to go home to New Orleans."

Lydia loved New Orleans, but it was not always the safest place to live. "I rather like it here in Reno. And Maya is adjusting very nicely."

"Maya is a child, she shouldn't have to adjust," Leon said. He reached into the inner pocket of his coat and pulled out an envelope. He handed it to her, but she didn't take it. He opened the envelope and took out folded paper, opened it and shoved it at her. She refused to look at it while her brain processed what Leon had just said. "Just sign this and we'll take Maya back to New Orleans, where she belongs." He took a pen out of his pocket and set it in front of her as though he simply expected her to pick it up and sign, just because he told her so. She studied him, realizing that was exactly what he expected her to do.

"No," she said firmly.

David gazed at her, surprise in his eyes. She felt a certain self-satisfaction knowing they'd never expected her to object.

"Don't be difficult, Lydia." Leon spoke to her as though she were a child. "This is the best for Maya."

"I'm what is best for Maya."

Leon frowned, fury filling his eyes. "Don't make us do this the hard way, Lydia. We'll enroll her in the Schubert Academy. She'll be with her friends. We're happy to give you visitation rights."

Lydia shoved the paper back at him. "There isn't a court in this land that will give you custody of my daughter."

Leon smiled thinly. "Lydia, don't be stupid. You think we don't know."

"Don't know what?" Puzzled, she could only stare at him.

"That you cheated on my father."

Her mouth fell open in surprise. "I beg your pardon?"

"Think of the scandal when the whole world finds out that Maya isn't our father's daughter."

"Really!" Lydia bit the inside of her cheek trying to stop the flare of pain at the accusation. How could they? "You would create a scandal to do what's best for Maya. The world will wonder why you want her so badly if she isn't even your sister."

"The world doesn't need to know," David put in. "She may not be a Montgomery by blood, but she is a Montgomery be association and needs to be raised properly."

"Like you two," Lydia said, bitterness welling inside her. She'd underestimated David and Leon.

Leon brushed her comment aside. "Think of the embarrassment your parents would suffer. Your father is considering running for a political office. How do you think the people of Louisiana would take the news that his only grandchild is another's man's child? This information would damage his campaign irreparably." Leon shoved the paperwork back at her.

Her father wanted to run for office? Her mother had never mentioned her father had political ambitions. Suddenly she wondered what their game was. "If I agreed to this, I assume you would also want control of her trust fund."

David smiled and appeared to relax, as though they had won and any arguments she presented were just part of the negotiation. "Of course, Lydia."

No matter that Mitchell had left them each a sizable amount, they wanted it all. She pushed to her feet and stood with her hands braced against the table leaning over them. "I never once cheated on my husband. Maya is his daughter."

"I have an affidavit, signed by your lover, Edmund de Lacy, claiming Maya as his daughter." Again Leon reached into his pocket and pulled out an envelope and waved it at her.

"I have no idea who Edmund de Lacy is," Lydia said.

"He knows you." David leered at her. "Apparently well enough to know about a certain mole."

Lydia glanced at Vanessa, who watched her quietly. "If I have to dig up my husband to prove how absurd you claim is, then you'll have to prove the same."

"What do you mean?" Leon asked, his eyes narrowing.

"I suggest we do DNA testing." All she needed was

their DNA and Maya's to prove they were related. That should satisfy any court.

David nodded. "That's fine. Leon and I will be happy to donate DNA to prove our familial relationship to Maya through our father. But don't depend on getting the results you think you'll get."

Vanessa stood and walked over to Leon. She took the envelope, opened it carefully and scanned the contents. "Gentlemen." She handed them a business card. "My client and I will be expecting to hear from your attorney at his earliest convenience." She gripped Lydia by the hand. "Come on, you have nothing more to say." She pulled Lydia out of the bar and out into the lobby to the elevators. "We have to talk, now."

Lydia could only nod, too stunned at David and Leon's absurd statement that Maya wasn't Mitchell's daughter. What did they think they would gain? They weren't going to shame her into signing the custody agreement. She had nothing to be ashamed of. And did they really think she was afraid of a scandal? So afraid she'd just sign to preserve the illusion that Maya was Mitchell's daughter? They had another think coming. As they stalked through the lobby to the elevator, Lydia gritted her teeth, ready for the fight to come.

Hunter stood at the bank of elevators waiting. Out of the corner of his eye, he saw Lydia walking toward him with a woman in tow. The woman was beautiful with dark brown hair pulled back into a tight bun at the base of her neck. She wore a cream-colored suit that perfectly complimented her caramel brown skin. A dark brown scarf was looped around her neck, providing another perfect color to compliment her dark brown eyes.

"I'm so angry." Lydia jabbed the up button even though it was already lit.

"Angry about what?" Hunter said.

She looked at him in surprise as though she'd just noticed him. She gestured at the two men leaving the lounge. "They think they can take my child away from me."

Hunter had already heard about Leon and David Montgomery from his grandmother, who had nothing nice to say about them.

The other woman intervened. "Let get somewhere private before we talk about this some more."

The elevator doors opened and Hunter allowed Lydia and the other woman to precede him. Once inside, Lydia tapped impatiently at the brass railing. Even in the short time he'd known her, he'd never seen her so agitated. He wanted to soothe her, but wasn't certain she wanted to be soothed.

The elevator reached the family floor, the doors slid open and Lydia pushed her way out and stalked down the hall to her suite. She swiped her room card and opened the door.

"Hello," the woman said to Hunter once they were inside the suite. "I'm Vanessa Peabody, Lydia's lawyer."

"Hunter Russell."

"Miss E. has spoken of you."

Miss E. sat on the sofa, a book in her hands. She looked up at their entrance. When her gaze shifted to Lydia, her eyes widened. "Things didn't go well with your meeting."

Lydia was so agitated she couldn't stay still. "How dare they? How dare they?" She shook herself as though trying to calm down. "I don't know how many times Mitchell bailed those two out of trouble. And you should see the women they date. And they think they can raise a child better than me. I may own a casino, which they seem to think is the next mortal sin, even though they use them for their own pleasure."

Miss E. patted the sofa next to her. "Lydia, sit down. You need to calm yourself. You're shouting and Maya is going to hear."

Lydia sat down and looked morosely at her hands. Hunter decided a glass of wine wouldn't hurt. He opened the bar fridge and found a bottle of Lydia's favorite pinot grigio and poured her a healthy amount. He handed her the glass, but she set it down on the side table. He poured a glass for Vanessa Peabody and his grandmother, but chose water for himself.

Vanessa Peabody related what had happened in the bar. Miss E. frowned and Hunter felt his grip on the water bottle tighten.

"That's it," Hunter said, his own anger rising to match Lydia's. "They're out. I will have them ejected from this hotel immediately."

Lydia nodded. Miss E. raised a hand. "No. You keep your friends close, but your enemies closer. We need them here to keep an eye on them."

"Exactly what do you mean to do?" Hunter asked his grandmother.

She frowned while she thought. "The people who work in this hotel will be cleaning their rooms and serving their food. We'll just let everyone know they are to be watched. And every move they make we will know about."

"We may have to offer hazard pay to the housekeeping staff," Lydia said with an angry laugh.

"Then we'll do that," Miss E. said calmly. "And a bonus to anyone who reports on them."

"I'm assigning a security detail to you and Maya." Hunter thought for a moment. "And I'm calling Scott." Scott Russell was Hunter's younger brother. He worked for a security firm in Washington, D.C. He might have some insight on how to protect Maya and Lydia.

Lydia covered her face with her hands. Her shoulders hunched and for a second she looked defeated. Then she rested her hands in her lap and straightened up, her head high. "I don't think they're going to do anything to Maya," she said. "They want to control the money Maya inherited."

Vanessa pulled a notebook and pen out of her purse. "Tell me about your late husband's will."

"My husband was worth nearly eight hundred million dollars. He left fifty million to David and Leon, fifty million to me and the bulk to Maya. She's worth approximately six hundred fifty million dollars and owns rental and commercial property in a number of different cities and a property development company headquartered in New Orleans."

Vanessa made notes. "Does your daughter have a stake in the casino as well?"

Lydia nodded. "Yes. Since she's only eight, I hold it in trust for her. Mitchell was always big about investing in property. He left a list of suggestions on how to invest her money and one suggestion was actually a casino. He considered casinos recession proof. Though I think he meant a casino in Lousiana and not here. But I thought, why not go where casinos are big business? So I came to Reno and met Miss E. So here I am and they are not taking my daughter."

When she smiled, her face lit up and Hunter found himself smiling with her. He wanted to protect her, to keep her safe. And Maya was becoming important to him, too.

"We need to look into their finances." Vanessa made a couple of notes in the notebook, a slight frown on her face.

"Mitchell has only been gone two years. David and

Leon couldn't possibly have gone through their inheritance already."

Vanessa sort of laughed. "You have no idea, Lydia, what people can do with a lot of money."

"What we really need is a plan." Hunter had already started making lists in his mind.

"Calling Scott is number one on your list," Miss E. said. "If anyone can think like the bad guys, it's Scott."

"Then we definitely need him," Vanessa said. "And who is he?"

"My brother," Hunter replied. And a badass himself, even though he'd never gotten into trouble, or at least trouble anyone could prove. As a child, he'd always thought Scott was like Teflon. Nothing stuck to him, no matter what mischief he got into. Hunter had taken the fall for him more than once.

"And get him here as quickly as you can," Miss E. added.

Hunter didn't think that would be a problem. The last time they'd spoken Scott had mentioned he was tired of his job and looking for a change. He pulled his cell out of his pocket and even though it was after midnight in Washington, D.C., Hunter knew his brother was probably up.

Scott answered on the first ring. "Yo, bro."

"Are you busy?" Hunter asked.

"Just watching a seventy-six-year-old senator getting his groove on with a twenty-one-year-old cheerleader from Georgetown University. All while his wife of fifty years is waiting at home thinking he's in a budget meeting."

"Not what I wanted to know," Hunter said. He'd have to have that image burned out of his mind.

"Yeah, that was my response. What's up?"

"You know how you've been wanting a change of jobs. Something a little closer to Grandma."

"I'm listening."

"I need you."

"I'm there." A short pause occurred and then Scott said, "A flight is leaving from Baltimore in few hours. I'm on it. I have to change planes in Chicago, but I should be there around noon."

"Text me your flight info and I'll pick you up," Hunter said, relieved to know Scott was coming. Scott was the security expert, not Hunter.

"See ya." Scott disconnected.

"He'll be here noon tomorrow," Hunter said.

Miss E. looked relieved.

Vanessa put her notebook away. "Then I'll be back tomorrow afternoon around three and we'll all talk again." She stood up and smoothed the front of her suit. "Until then, Lydia, if your stepsons approach you, make sure you have someone with you. Do not let them force you into being alone with them. I'll start the ball rolling on the DNA testing."

Lydia stood to walk Vanessa to the door. Vanessa hugged her. "Stop worrying. That's my job now."

Lydia closed the door after Vanessa, leaned against it and burst into tears.

Chapter 3

Miss E. jumped up and put her arms around Lydia. "It's going to be all right."

"This is not going to affect Maya in a positive way. During my marriage, I walked a fine line trying to get along with David and Leon. Maybe I should just pay them. After all, it's the money they want."

Hunter held up his hand. "Whoa. There is no chance you will lose your daughter; you're not paying them a dime."

"I want them to go away." Lydia felt crushed beneath the weight of David and Leon's threat.

"Give them money and they'll just keep coming back. Now that their daddy is gone, they see you as their next ATM. You have to shut them down. Permanently." Hunter wasn't about to let Lydia be blackmailed.

"Maya thinks her half brothers love her."

"And you're not going to disabuse her of that," Miss E. said firmly.

"Somehow, someway, she's going to find out what's going on and I'm afraid of what it will do to her."

"Children are more resilient than we think," Miss E. replied. "She'll be hurt, but in the long run, she'll be okay. She has you."

Hunter clenched his hands. He wanted to beat the crap

out of those two men. They were tearing apart a good woman and making her life miserable.

Lydia wiped her eyes. Even though she was in the middle of a meltdown her posture was perfect. Where did that thought come from? Hunter wondered.

Lydia sat down, a vulnerable look on her face. He wondered if she were a little too delicate to handle this situation.

"You are not going to let them defeat you." Miss E. patted Lydia's hand. "Now, you're going to get a good night's sleep and tomorrow, we're going to put on our war paint."

Lydia smiled. Hunter wanted to gather her up in his arms. The urge to protect her was so strong, he took a step forward before he stopped. He wanted to kiss her. That thought shocked him. He'd avoided romantic entanglements for a long time. The women he'd dated over the years just didn't have long-term potential, yet in a couple days, he was already half in love with Lydia. Usually he didn't care for fragile, frail-looking women. But something about her brought out all his need to safeguard her from life. Though, he suspected she didn't need protecting as much as he wanted to think she did.

Miss E. stood and Hunter followed her. "If you need anything," he said, "I'm just down the hall."

"Thank you, Hunter, Miss E." She smiled at them and Hunter's heart skipped a beat.

Out in the hall, Hunter walked his mother to the elevator. "Do you think she'll be all right?"

"She's a lot stronger than she thinks she is. And she's got us."

"We don't really know her."

"I know her," his grandmother said. "She's a good person."

"This is not someone sitting across the poker table from you while you're plotting to take their money."

"True. I can tell what type of person she is because of her daughter. Maya is sweet, engaging child, who's going to start breaking hearts pretty soon. She's polite, fun and smart. You don't get to have a daughter like that if you're not a good person, too."

Hunter was impressed. Miss E. had a tendency toward cynicism. "I can see you really like Maya and her mother."

Miss E. pushed the down button on the elevator. "You like her, too."

"Maya's a cute little thing." Like her mother, Maya brought out his protective instincts.

"I'm not talking about Maya," Miss E. said.

Maybe it was time to be a little evasive. He liked Lydia a lot. Maybe more than a lot. "What's not to like?"

"Indeed." The elevator doors slid open and Miss E. stepped into the cabin.

"Good night, Miss E." Hunter kissed her on the cheek. She smiled at him as the elevator door closed.

Hunter waited at the baggage carousel for his brother. Scott's plane had landed ten minutes ago and passengers were filing in. Scott should have been one of the first off the plane. He almost always flew first class. Instead, he was almost last.

Hunter gazed fondly at his brother. Scott was tall and muscular. Close-cropped black hair framed his face and his erect posture was a testament to his years in the army. He never seemed to leave the military behind.

"Good to see you, Hunter." Scott put out his hand and Hunter grabbed it and pulled him into a hug.

"Back at ya, bro," Hunter said. "It's been too long."

"I see Miss E. is getting into trouble again."

"She won a casino in a poker game."

"So I heard." Scott's laughter was a deep rumble that had everyone turning to look at him. "I'm not sure how I feel about that."

"Wait till you see it. It's a Spanish hacienda on steroids. I'm always surprised the staff doesn't hand out capes and matador hats the minute we walk through the door."

Scott grabbed his duffel bag off the carousel and followed Hunter out into the afternoon heat. The sky was clear, brilliant blue. The summer sun had baked the ground to a hard shell. Parched-looking trees lined the sidewalks and straggly grass grew between the cracks in the asphalt.

"What's the situation?" Scott asked once they were in the car, the AC cranked up on high and the car moving out of the parking lot. Heat waves shimmered in the distance.

"One of Miss E.'s partners in the casino is being blackmailed by her stepsons. They want custody of her daughter and are willing to smear the family name to get it."

"Have you reported this to the police?"

"It's not really a police matter."

"When is blackmail not a police matter?"

"Right now, it's only at the threat stage." The police would consider it a civil matter.

"Start from the beginning," Scott ordered.

Hunter did. By the time they got to the hotel, Scott knew every detail. Hunter felt a weight lift. The Montgomery boys weren't going to get away with anything, not with Scott on the job.

"Lydia is more concerned about what damage the custody suit will do to her daughter." Hunter pulled into the parking lot adjacent to the casino and sat for a moment looking at it.

"Then we need to find a way to make them drop the suit."

"That will be easier said than done. There's a lot of money at stake here. Money those two want, and from what I'm seeing they'll do anything to get their hands on it." Hopefully not to the extent that Maya and Lydia would be collateral damage. But just seeing those two walking through the casino as though they already owned it set Hunter's teeth on edge.

"Wow! This is beautiful," Scott said with a low whistle.

"Yeah." Hunter studied the hotel, with its rounded balconies and Spanish mosaic tiles. "Miss E. has it in mind to leave us all a legacy."

"I don't think I want it. How do Kenzie and Donovan feel about being handed a legacy like this?" Scott spread his hands wide.

Hunter shrugged. "Haven't talked to them again. Miss E. called, but didn't tell me what they said. Structurally, the building is sound. A little paint and spackle and it could be the jewel of Reno." Hunter turned off the car. "Come on, Miss E. is waiting for us."

Lydia stepped out of the elevator. Every time she entered the lobby, she paused to look around for David or Leon. Too often one of them was sitting where he could see the elevators. She didn't know they had so much patience. Though they kept a certain distance from her, she was always aware that they watched her, distracting her from her thoughts.

She wanted to get started on the spa, to make it an island of serenity in the midst of the chaos that was Reno. Her notebook was never far from her hand as she sketched ideas, made notes about colors and websites she checked. The spa was all about pampering and it was going to be the best in the whole United States.

Miss E. stood in a small alcove just off the main lobby.

A woman towered over her in a manner Lydia at first thought was threatening. Lydia started toward Miss E., when the woman suddenly turned and stalked away. Lydia knew her. She vaguely recalled the woman was Jasper's daughter. She'd been in the gallery, sitting across from Jasper during the poker game. The woman had looked angry and kept darting glances at Jasper as though he were the enemy. Once the game had been won, Lydia had dismissed her when she'd angrily left.

"Miss E., wasn't that Jasper's daughter? She was at the poker game. She sat in the gallery with Jasper and I."

"She's none too happy about the change in ownership." Miss E.'s eyes narrowed and her cheeks were a little pale. Her hands had formed into fists.

"What's she doing here?"

"Trying to steal from me." Miss E. watched as the woman exited through the sliding glass doors after one last hard glare over her shoulder.

"I don't understand." Lydia frowned at her.

"Don't worry. I'll take care of it. You have enough to worry about."

Hunter walked into the lobby with a taller man, whose face resembled his enough for Lydia to know this had to be Scott. He was a nice-looking man, his skin a lighter shade of brown than Hunter's and an alert look to him. His posture was ramrod straight with wide, muscular shoulders and strong hands. His short hair was in a military cut. He carried a green canvas duffel bag and walked across the lobby toward Miss E. as though he owned the moment.

"Miss E." Scott kissed his grandmother on the cheek.

Miss E. threw her arms around him and hugged him, affection on her face. "Scott. Okay, now I have two little chicks back in the nest."

The pleasure and love on Scott's and Hunter's faces

told her how much they loved their grandmother. For a second, Lydia felt sad. Her own parents had not given her such unconditional love. Their love and approval had always come with strings attached.

Scott laughed. "Miss E., you're always the optimist." He turned to Lydia. "You must be Lydia."

She smiled and nodded, a little intimidated by him. He took her hand and squeezed it reassuringly. "You and I need to talk," Scott continued. "I want to know everything about your relationship to your stepchildren."

"I don't have a relationship with them. They consider me an interloper, who took their mother's rightful place."

"Did you?"

"Mitchell and Gloria had been divorced for years before I came on the scene. Her loyalties to Mitchell were… shall we say, suspect." She tried to speak kindly of Gloria. Lydia's mother had always insisted that gossip was beneath the dignity of a lady. Mitchell, himself, had never said an unkind word about his ex-wife. Lydia got all the gossip, more than she wanted to know, from people who had worked for Mitchell and had disliked Gloria intensely.

"Delicately put," Scott murmured.

"I only met her a few times, and I couldn't gauge her." Lydia felt uncomfortable talking about Gloria. And frankly, she wasn't surprised by Leon and David's ploy. Even though they acted unconcerned about the way the money was split, she knew they had been angry right after the reading of the will. Even Lydia had been surprised. She had not expected Mitchell to leave the bulk of his estate to Maya with Lydia as executer.

"Right. Let me get settled and we'll meet in your suite in an hour. We have a lot to go over and I need more information."

"Vanessa Peabody is my lawyer, and she's coming at three."

"Our meeting won't take long."

Hunter and Scott walked off with Hunter telling his brother they would be bunking together.

"He's going to probe into every aspect of my life, isn't he?" Lydia said to Miss E.

"Sweetie, how much trouble have you gotten into in the past?"

"I'm not perfect," Lydia objected. "When I was seven years old, I stole a cherry red lipstick from Mr. Benoit's drug store."

"Oh, the horror," Miss E. said with a twinkle in her eyes. "Hunter stole a police car when he was fourteen. I always suspected Scott had something to do with it, too, but I could never pin anything on him. He's very cunning. The police chief was a friend of mine and Hunter spent six months washing police cars every weekend."

Lydia laughed. She tried to imagine Hunter as a juvenile delinquent. Interestingly it made her like him even more. Her heart hammered in her chest thinking about him being bad. She'd bet her last dollar he could charm himself out of any situation, if he so chose.

"Now that Scott was a sneaky kid. I know he was involved in a number of activities, but I could never catch him or prove anything."

"Should I be nervous that he wants to help me?"

Miss E. patted her cheek. "No, dear, you should be grateful."

Lydia glanced at her watch. "I should get upstairs. Maya's tutor will be leaving soon and we need to have a talk about Maya's progress."

"When you're ready I'll take her off your hands while

you talk to Scott," Miss E. said. "I thought we might do something interesting."

"Like what?"

"I have a friend who has a ranch just north of Reno. I thought we might look at ponies." Miss E. grinned in delight.

"I'm going be purchasing that child a horse, aren't I?"

Miss E. patted Lydia's cheek. "She's a wonderful, active child and you are invested in keeping her out of trouble. When my grandchildren were her age, I had them so occupied in sports, they seldom had time to think, much less get in trouble. Though they still managed a few misadventures."

Lydia narrowed her eyes. "I've never been very sportsminded." Her parents had wanted different things for her. The most sport she'd ever done was roller skating at a local rink and that had only been a few times.

Miss E. smiled. "I think sports for kids is a very good thing. For me, it's not about the competition of good gamesmanship."

A couple with two children walked into the lobby. They trailed suitcases on wheels. The little boy loudly announced he wanted to be a cowboy and the mother simply shook her head, looking frazzled. They approached the desk and started to check in.

Lydia was amazed that despite the lack of amenities people still came to stay at the *Mariposa* when they could go elsewhere. Circus Circus was a good choice for families.

The sounds from the casino reached out into the lobby. She could hear the clanking of dishes from the café. Suddenly an idea for the spa started to coalesce in her mind. Spanish architecture was based on the influence of the Moors. She had an idea for billowing curtains, intricate mosaic tile floors and overstuffed sofas. She headed toward her office, anxious to get as many of her ideas written down and sketched out, feeling as happy as she'd ever been since before Mitchell passed away.

Lydia removed the art from the walls and replaced them with some of her own in an attempt to make the suite more personable. Having her own possessions around her gave her a strong sense of comfort. She rearranged the furniture to make the foyer and living room feel a little less cavernous.

For the deck, she requested plants to break up the long, straight line of the pond and add a bit of color. The pond was barely a foot deep, but koi flashed back and forth, hiding under the large leaves of the water lilies in the brightness of the early afternoon sun.

The suite was quiet without Maya's constant chatter. Lydia had arranged for her to take an extra tutoring session in a meeting room down the hall from the suite so she would be gone when the meeting with Vanessa happened. The tutor had been advised not to turn Maya over to anyone but Lydia, and Hunter had posted a security guard outside the room just in case. Lydia didn't want Maya accidentally overhearing their planning session. Maya liked Miss Weston. She made learning fun and Maya soaked up knowledge like a sponge.

She sat at the desk in a corner of the living room, more at ease now that Maya would be ready for school here. She could get a bit of work done before her meeting with Vanessa.

Hunter had worked out a plan for the building of the spa and Lydia read through it several times. A survey team had been hired to measure the open areas around the hot springs. Hunter had the job of talking to the building department to get the necessary information he would need to apply for building permits.

Lydia's job was to start putting together color schemes and look for samples of carpet and tile. She'd already been to a variety of home improvement stores to collect paint chips that were currently spread across the top of her desk.

She couldn't seem to focus. Her mind kept skittering away from her task to her stepsons. Despite Vanessa's assurance that she wouldn't lose custody, she couldn't take the risk. She wasn't a gambler like Miss E., who seemed to understand the cards in some sort of psychic manner.

David and Leon scared her. She'd met Leon's children and they weren't nice children. She knew all teenagers went through stages of defiance, but his children had taken the stage to new levels.

A knock sounded on the door and she rose to answer it, opening the door to Hunter. The more she saw him, the more she had this queer little lurch inside that left her heart pounding and her palms damp. He made her feel all gooey and uncomfortable.

"What's wrong?" he asked.

She sighed. "I know everyone says that my chances of losing Maya are slim to none, but I don't even want slim."

Hunter shook his head. "We're not going to let that happen."

"How can you be so sure?"

"Scott is digging up dirt on them right now. No one is going to look at you and look at them and think you're a terrible mother. You have a happy kid."

Again, Lydia's thoughts went back to Leon's angry children. She doubted they would ever be happy. Their mothers weren't happy. All three of Leon's baby mamas had been minimum wage earners, and even though the estate paid each one of them a generous amount each month, they were never satisfied nor did they seem to have anything left at the end of the day. Was anger something in their genes, something they'd never overcome?

"You need to stop worrying so much. You're a good mother, Lydia," Hunter repeated. "David and Leon may make things uncomfortable for a time, but they don't have a chance of getting custody."

But she couldn't stop worrying. Another knock sounded on the door and Lydia opened it to find Vanessa and Scott in the hall. They entered. Vanessa immediately sat on the sofa to open her briefcase and pull out a folder, her laptop and a long box with DNA Kit stamped on the side. Scott also opened his laptop, and Lydia found herself tensing.

"Lydia," Scott said, "I started things in motion to get a thorough background check. I should have results in a few days. And I want to put security cameras in their suite. Will you let me?"

"I don't know about that," Vanessa said with a side glance at Scott. "They have an expectation of privacy in their suite."

"It would give us some idea about what they're up to so we can plan accordingly," Scott said.

"I'm uncomfortable with that," Lydia said.

"Why?" Scott asked.

"It's so…unseemly."

"Unseemly! These two lowlifes want to take your kid."

Lydia mused over his suggestion. She glanced at Hunter. "He's a pit bull."

"I'm your pit bull," Scott answered with a grin.

"What would you do?" Lydia asked Miss E.

"To keep my kids? Anything."

Lydia would do anything, too, but some things just seemed wrong. "But would this information be admissible in court?"

Vanessa thought for a moment. "Depends on the judge and how we present our argument, but I'm going to go with a no. Though knowing what they're doing does give us an advantage."

"They've only been here two days," Hunter put in, "and they've already brought in what I will euphemistically call 'dates.' We have them on tape. I should think it would give a judge some idea of their character."

Lydia closed her eyes, her thoughts whirling. When she opened them to look at Hunter, she couldn't think how to frame her question.

"Listen," Hunter said patiently, "we won't do anything that makes you uncomfortable."

His eyes looked so concerned, and she was grateful. "At this point, I'm uncomfortable with putting security cameras in the suite. I think we can get enough information about them without doing something like that."

"Okay then," Scott said, "no security cameras in their suite."

She glanced around and realized no one was judging her for her decision. They accepted her decision without argument and she suddenly felt good. Her parents had always questioned her decisions and usually she would change her mind to please them. As much as Mitchell indulged her, he'd never asked her opinion about anything. He'd assumed she didn't have one. She felt like she belonged right here, right now, with these people, who all looked at her with concern in their eyes. And for the first time in her whole life, she'd felt like she had a real family, one who treated her like a grownup capable of making mature decisions. She liked being treated like a thinking, intelligent person.

The conversation drifted around her while she thought about David and Leon. Would they really claim Maya to be illegitimate to forward their claims?

"I'll be talking to hotel security in an hour to discuss setting up remote surveillance on them," Scott said. "I want all their actions on tape."

"I've done a little digging," Vanessa said, "and found out they do like their gambling. And they like their girls and their alcohol."

"And," Miss E. added, "they like messing with the hotel staff. They've alienated everyone they've come into contact with."

"We can use that," Vanessa said, typing furiously on her laptop. "I want everyone on your staff who comes into contact with them to document the encounter. This indicates character, or lack of."

Lack of, Lydia thought with a half smile. She didn't realize she was staring at Hunter until he raised an eyebrow at her. She felt heat blossom on her face. She liked his character. And wished…she didn't know what she wished for. She had to stop thinking about how much she liked Hunter and concentrate on Maya's safety.

Focus, she sternly ordered herself. Focus on the problem at hand. She'd only been a widow for two years. Thinking about Hunter was improper. But why, why was liking him now considered improper? Her mother had stressed at Mitchell's funeral that her future behavior had to be above reproach. She wasn't supposed to taint her name, and yet she'd run away to Reno and unexpectedly found herself the owner of a casino. David and Leon made a career out of tarnishing their family name, while her parents held her to a much higher standard.

"Lydia," Hunter said. "Are you all right?"

She nodded. "I was just thinking about things better left alone."

"What kind of things?"

"The past," she admitted.

"Nothing good comes from thinking about the past," Miss E. said. "You need to let it go. You have one hell of a fight in front of you, sweetie."

"I know the odds arc in your favor," Hunter stressed, "but I don't think David and Leon are bright enough to know that."

"And that makes them dangerous," Scott put in.

Lydia was too restless to relax. She left Maya with Miss E., who was teaching her the art of the inside straight after they went to look at horses. Miss E. stressed that poker taught two very important lessons—self-discipline and reading body language. Lydia wasn't certain how she felt about her daughter learning poker, she did know that the lessons learned would last her the rest of her life. Poker was a game of strategy and would teach Maya how to think and puzzle through challenges. Lydia's grandfather had taught her how to play chess, but to her chess was just a game. Not until later in her life did she realize chess was a game of strategy and since she didn't play as well as she thought she should, she felt she'd wasted her grandfather's lessons.

Without realizing it, Lydia found herself at the hot springs, dangling her feet in the warm water, breathing in the mineral smell and letting her stress drain away.

She didn't want her daughter being raised by anyone but her. How Leon and David thought they could convince a judge to turn Maya over to them puzzled her. She didn't doubt for a minute that it was the money they were after, but to use Maya so callously said a lot about their character, or, as Vanessa said, lack of. If not for Maya, she would have written them a check for whatever they wanted. The problem was they wanted it all. Maya was a child with a bright future and she had no doubt her daughter could make a success out of herself with nothing but her own grit and determination, but she was going to give her child every advantage she could. That included a happy future. They were grown men who'd already wasted their future.

Mitchell had been generous in providing for Leon's children, but she knew Leon was frustrated by the iron-clad trust he couldn't touch. Every penny needed to be accounted for and Everest had an accountant who did nothing but work on the trust and deflect Leon's demands. And once the children turned twenty-five, the trust reverted back to Maya, which was another thing that galled Leon. Which Lydia thought was kind of odd. But she'd never questioned Everest about why Mitchell had written the trust the way he had.

"Lydia, why are you out here alone?" Hunter sat down next to her.

"Maya is having her poker lesson and I didn't want to hover."

"Self-discipline and body language skills," Hunter said with a chuckle.

"She called them life lessons." Hunter took his shoes off, rolled up his pant legs and put his feet into the water with a little sigh.

"So she taught you to play poker, too."

"All of us," he said.

"How do you use your life lessons in your occupation?"

Hunter rolled up his socks and put them inside his shoes. "I restore old buildings to their former glamour. The problem with some owners is that they don't understand the importance of being accurate. Like the Painted Ladies. The colors they were originally were always bright and cheerful, colors we consider ticky-tacky today, but were appropriate to that style. And I can tell when someone is going to be difficult or accommodating. I know just how much I can say to talk a difficult client into doing what needs to be done, and I learned by controlling my reactions and reading their body language. I'm not just an architect. A lot of time, I'm a therapist."

Lydia tilted her head, thinking about what he'd just said. Mitchell had lived in the Garden District house where his ancestors had originally been slaves. He'd even searched for the original furniture and found as many pieces as he could. He'd spent millions of dollars restoring that house to its former glory and he'd been incredibly proud of the fact that he'd come to own the house his ancestors slaved at.

She had never liked the house. It was cluttered and cold and whatever character it had seemed submerged beneath layers of pain. She never felt comfortable. Living in the house was like sitting down in a wobbly, two-hundred-year old chair. If it broke, she had to call a specialist to repair it.

She didn't sell the house because it was Maya's heritage, but the minute the will had been read and probated, she'd packed her bags and rented a house in the French Quarter. She'd turned the Garden District house into a museum and allowed the local historical society to use it for tours. Hunter would have had a field day restoring that old house.

"Why Reno?" Hunter shifted to get comfortable on the hard rock.

"Because it was so unexpected," Lydia said. "All my life I've done what was expected of me. I was sent to the right schools, the right college. I earned the right degrees with the best grades. I married the right man and ate at the right restaurants and supported the right charities, because all those things were expected of me. When Mitchell died, my expectations of the right life died with him, and I thought, what the hell. If life was going to shake me up, I would shake life up right back."

"So you came to Reno when you could have gone to Paris, London or even New York."

"I thought about going to Paris, but that would be expected of me. No one expected me to show up in the 'biggest little city' in the world and win a casino in a poker game." Her parents had been appalled at her when she announced she was leaving. Her mother argued with her about appearances and tarnishing her upstanding family's image. She refused to listen. Mitchell's death freed her. He'd left her a generous amount of money to live her life and that was what she planned to do—live her life according to her rules.

"Now that I get," Hunter said.

"Why are you here?"

"I volunteered," he said with a chuckle. "When this is done, I'll head back to San Francisco and pick up where I left off."

"So you think," she replied. Miss E. was a spider and once she had someone in her web, that person was caught. "Your grandmother has you exactly where she wants you—back in the fold."

"In the back of my head, I know you're right," Hunter said with another laugh. "But I'm going to go right on pretending I'm a grown man and continue with my life."

She joined him in laughter. "Five minutes after meeting Miss E., I knew she was going to keep me in her life forever."

"Your parents were pretty controlling, from what you've said. Miss E. is just another form of control."

That was a fair statement. "I thought we were just going to be friends. I had no idea we were going to be business partners, and I'll be honest, this was one of the best decisions I've ever made." She splashed at the water with her feet too aware of the warmth of his body next to her.

"Miss E. is like that, helping you come to the right conclusion, which is right in line with hers."

"You're being kind of harsh about your grandmother."

"I've known her longer than you have," he said with a grin.

They fell into silence. A cool wind blew in down the side of the mountain and Lydia shivered. He put an arm around her and she found herself leaning into his warmth. She wasn't expecting him to kiss her, but his lips on hers were warm and inviting. His kiss teased and excited her. She felt a tingle all the way down to her toes.

She pushed him away and scrambled to her feet and fled to the hotel without a backward look. She'd finally kissed him and she'd loved it. Yet at the same time she felt a sense of disloyalty to Mitchell. His kiss had never excited her like this. Not once during their marriage did he make her feel dizzy and out of control.

Chapter 4

Hunter stood in the center of the lobby watching as the workman assembled their scaffolding and set out barriers to keep incoming patrons safe. They were fixing some water damage discovered when a painting had been removed for cleaning.

Lydia was at a low point in her life and he felt like a jerk, taking advantage of her. His kiss had surprised him probably more than Lydia. But something about her made him ache to protect her, to keep her safe, to keep her for himself. Kissing her was going about it the wrong way.

The elevator door opened and Lydia walked out. She took one look at him and scurried away in a different direction, avoiding him.

"What did you do to Lydia?" Miss E. poked him in the ribs with one finger.

"Nothing," Hunter protested.

"I can smell guilt from a mile away and you reek of it." She crossed her arms over her chest.

"You know I'm a grown man, right?"

"Even before you came to live with me, I changed your dirty diapers. I had to take your crap then, not anymore."

He couldn't lie to his grandmother. She had his number and having her look at him the way she was right now made feel him five years old again. When did grandparents get around to not doing that anymore?

"I kissed Lydia," he mumbled.

"You what?" She poked him again.

"I kissed Lydia."

"Why would you do something like that?" With fists balanced on each hip, she glared up at him with her bull terrier look designed to put him in his place and keep him there.

Because he'd been dying to kiss her since he'd first seen her. "It seemed like the right thing to do…at that moment," he half whispered.

Eyebrows arched over intense brown eyes, she glared at him. "Lydia has enough on her plate. She doesn't need you sniffing around."

"You make me sound like a dog."

"You're a man," she said, one eyebrow raised. "Which means you should just know better."

He thought again about the kiss, the softness of her lips, the faint scent of her perfume and the desire to protect her. "She seems so delicate."

"Hmph," Miss E. snapped.

"What does that mean exactly?"

"It means what it means," she said.

Great. Now his grandmother was being cryptic.

A bus pulled up to the front door and opened to disgorge a line of seniors, who entered the lobby and made a beeline to the casino. The Mariposa was on the senior gambling route. Mostly the casino pulled in locals who preferred a smaller casino to a larger, more tourist themed one.

Thirty-seven elderly men and women trooped by in groups, laughing and talking. One woman held a roll of quarters in her hand. Another carried a round cookie tin that rattled. A man thumped by with his cane, gnarled fingers grabbing the handle tightly.

"Is big bad John doing his magic act today?" the old man asked Miss E.

"Yes, he is." Miss E. pointed at the casino and the elderly man nodded and thumped inside.

Once the elderly patrons were gone, Hunter turned to his grandmother. "You think I should stay away from Lydia."

She gave him that look that used to shrink his guts when he'd been a kid. He had to stand his ground.

"You're going to do what you're going to do."

"I don't understand," he said in exasperation. His grandmother was so…so difficult to interpret.

"That's your problem," she stated simply and walked away.

"Having granny problems?" Scott asked from behind Hunter.

"Having woman problems," Hunter half snarled.

"I'll admit, she's beautiful," Scott said.

Hunter glared at his brother, holding in a spurt of jealousy. Scott had always had a way of getting women. Something about him just made them want to take care of him. He didn't want his brother looking at Lydia. Scott had his own woman, he needed to leave Hunter's alone.

"Your job is to keep her safe," Hunter said, trying to keep the snarl out of his tone.

Scott's eyes lit with amusement. "And what's your job?"

"My job is to…is…my job." Hunter spread his hands wide to take in the scaffolding being assembled, the workers repairing.

"Miss E. tried to warn you off, didn't she?" Scott said.

"She's protecting her investment."

"No, she's not," Scott replied. "Miss E. has plans."

Miss E. always had plans and woe to anyone who didn't fall in line. "I don't know what her plans are."

"We'll find out soon enough," Scott said.

Hunter shrugged. Of all the grandchildren, Scott was the most like Miss E. He was manipulative, secretive and liked being a behind the scenes puppet-master. If anyone could find out what Miss E. planned it would be Scott.

Scott glanced at his watch. "I've got to go. I have a meeting with those people you laughingly call security here. So far, I've been able to swipe two thousand in merchandise from the gallery stores, pick-pocketed two gamblers and discovered gaps in security I could drive a herd of T. rexes through."

"Why did you pick people's pockets?" Hunter demanded, thinking his brother was setting them up for a lawsuit.

"Two reasons," Scott replied, unperturbed. "One, pick-pockets working the floor is one of things security is supposed to be looking for. Two, I made a detailed description of everything in each wallet before I turned it in to lost and found. I want to make sure the lost wallets find their way back to the proper owners with everything intact."

"How are you going to find that out?"

"I have my ways."

"You're checking out the staff security with lost and found, too." Hunter was impressed with his brother. Scott thought of things nobody else did. He was sneaky that way.

Scott nodded. "All I can say is that the security here is sub-par and that's being polite."

"If you weren't my brother and working for the good guys, you'd make me nervous at your pride in all of this."

Scott shrugged. "Best way to improve the system?"

Hunter didn't answer. He watched his brother push open a door next to the check-in desk and head into the administrative offices.

* * *

Lydia walked into the lobby from the desert heat, two of Scott's security men unobtrusively flanking her and Maya. He had assured her that they would be enormously discreet and she would barely notice them.

Coolness surrounded her and dried the sweat trickling down her back even though the walk from the car had only been a couple of minutes. She held Maya's hand and listened to her daughter chatter about ballet lessons and her future riding lessons. Miss E. had found a stable that taught riding and Maya was excited. She would be starting her lessons in a week and rattled on and on about the ponies Ms. E. had taken her to see.

Scaffolding blocked their way and Lydia darted to the left, keeping to the path outlined by glaringly orange cones. Hunter stood in the center of the lobby, arms crossed over his chest as he watched the workmen as they plastered the wall. Lydia suggested they find someone to paint a mural in that spot instead of putting the painting back. All she had to do was decide what the mural would be.

While Maya had been at her lesson, Lydia had taken the time to head to a carpet store and pick up some samples of good quality commercial carpet in the colors she thought would best compliment the paint she'd chosen. Miss E. had approved the colors and once Hunter finished the blueprints with room sizes, she would start figuring out what furniture she wanted and where it needed to go along with deciding how the various massage rooms would be decorated. She planned to visit some of the different spas in Reno to see how they achieved the calm serenity that made spas so popular.

Hunter glanced at her. Her first impulse was to avoid him as she'd been doing all day, the kiss foremost in her mind, but instead, she walked up to him, Maya trailing her and looking around curiously while the two security men stationed themselves at a discreet distance. "You look very serious," Lydia said.

"I just had a long conversation with my brother."

"About?"

He told her about Scott's thefts and security's ineffectiveness.

"How horrible," Lydia replied. "What are we going to do?"

"Leave it to Scott. He'll fix it. That's his specialty."

"Yes," Lydia said with a quick glance at Maya's security detail. Maya had something in her hand and was showing the security guard. He nodded cordially, but didn't relax his security. She was surprised how well Maya accepted the two men who overlooked her every move.

The elevator doors at the end of the lobby slid open to reveal Leon and David. Lydia tensed. She'd managed to avoid them since the night in the lounge. And with the new security measures in place, they'd ceased stalking her.

David continued on into the casino. Leon caught sight of her and Maya. He walked across the lobby, dodging casino patrons, and squatted down in front of Maya. The security guard immediately tensed. Lydia quickly crossed the lobby to stand behind Maya.

"Hey, little sister," Leon said. "Have a kiss for your big brother?"

Lydia wanted to drag Maya away, but Maya did have a level of affection for her half brothers, even if they were considerably older than her.

She gave him a peck on the cheek. "Hello, Leon."

The two security guards went on high alert, shifting their stance, their eyes wary. Leon didn't seem to notice them.

"How's your mom treating you? Has she spanked you today?"

Even Maya looked surprised and then she laughed. "Mommy doesn't do that."

"Oh. Does she lock you in the closet?"

Lydia frowned. "Leon, that's inappropriate."

He gave her an innocent look. "Just checking on my little sister's welfare."

Hunter stepped up to Leon. "Leon, I hear you like the blackjack tables."

Leon stood, giving Hunter a superior look. "I don't think your dealers are to be trusted."

"Thank you for your input. You know we're revamping the resort. Every piece of information you can give me is helpful."

Leon snorted. "Your housekeeping staff is abominable. They never leave enough towels or soap samples. And two times the maid made the bed, but didn't change the sheets."

"All you have to do is ask for more towels," Hunter said.

Leon snorted again. "I have filed more complaints about this place in the first couple of days of my stay than any other hotel I've ever stayed in."

"So you like to file complaints."

"I expect compliance and respect when I ask for something. And I don't appear to be getting any of that from the staff in this hotel." He glanced at Lydia as though his discomfort was her fault.

Hunter rocked back on his heels. Lydia was grateful he'd shifted Leon's attention from Maya. She wanted to grab Maya and flee, but worried if she did it would draw Leon's attention back. So she stood, trying to look unobtrusive as she edged her way closer to the security team, who had stepped forward to flank her, their eyes attentive.

She never felt safe around Leon. Even when Mitchell

was alive, Leon worried her with the way he'd look at her as though she belonged in his bed rather than his father's. He'd groped her once and she'd stabbed his hand with a fork she happened to be holding. He never done that again, but she knew he wanted to hurt her back.

"One of the most important lessons my grandmother ever taught my siblings and me is that being 'nice' goes a long way toward getting what you want."

Leon sneered. Lydia snickered and put her hand over her mouth. Leon darted an angry glance at her. "It's your fault."

"What's my fault?" Lydia wasn't sure she wanted an answer.

"The reason we had to come to this fake cowboy wilderness is because of you," Leon said. "If you'd stayed in New Orleans like a proper woman, I wouldn't have had to trudge after you."

Lydia opened her mouth to say something, but Hunter held up his hand. "A good little woman." He pointed his finger at Lydia. "Shame on you, Lydia, for wanting to be independent, having your own life, setting a good example for Maya. Why ever would you give up a life of servitude to your stepson?"

Lydia felt a giggle in the back of her throat. She repressed it hard knowing Leon would hate her even more if she laughed at him. "I'm so sorry for wanting a better life."

Leon's mouth gaped open like a fish.

"Now if you'll excuse me." She put her hands over Maya's ears. "I'm going to spank Maya for no reason and lock her in a closet with no dinner. Assuming I can find a closet that locks. Of course I'm kidding, Maya is impeccably mannered, always polite and rarely needs correction." Unlike her brothers.

"I am, you know," Maya said to Leon with a wide smile.

"You really don't need to worry about me, Leon." She fluttered her eyes at Leon the same way Lydia used to flutter her eyes at Mitchell when she wanted something.

Lydia hid a smile. She took Maya's hand and walked her to the elevators, the security detail on her heels.

Hunter watched Lydia enter the elevator. He turned to Leon.

"Interesting play, Mr. Montgomery. Can I call you Leon?"

Leon's eyes narrowed. "I don't know what you mean."

"You have no hope in hell of getting custody of that child unless you prove Lydia's an unfit mother."

Leon glared at Hunter. "And what mother takes her child away from everything she knows to live some wild life in some desert city like Reno, Nevada."

Hunter studied the mother man. "That argument doesn't hold a lot of water. After all, there are a lot of mothers already living in Reno and their ability to mother isn't being called into question because they live here."

"You don't know anything."

"I know plenty," Hunter said. "I know Reno is considered one of the safest cities in the United States and has one of the better educational systems." Not that Hunter knew for sure. He was making this up as he went along. He didn't think Leon was going to research the city anyway. "And I know a happy kid when I see one."

"Maya is just pretending," Leon growled.

"She's too young to pretend. And I can tell when some bozo is hunting for straws."

He reached out to push Hunter away. Hunter grabbed his hand. "You are a soft, weak little man. Your best bet is not to start something I'm going to have to finish."

Leon jerked away and stomped toward the casino.

"You bully, you," Miss E. said. "I'm so ashamed of you."

Hunter whirled around, wondering where she'd come from. "He's lucky that's as far as I took it. I wanted to wring his scrawny little chicken neck."

"Losing your temper isn't going to help Lydia."

"When did we take on this family drama?" Hunter asked.

"Lydia has become a part of this family," Miss E. responded. "She needs us. And we're going to do what we can to keep her safe and our family together."

"There is no hope in hell that that doofus would ever win custody of a child."

"You never know. Just is unpredictable." Miss E. glanced at the entrance to the casino. "I read an article where several states in this great country allow rapists to visit their children derived from the rape. Any court that thinks that is in the best interests of the child is just as capable of giving custody of Maya to an incompetent half brother. We're going to do this right and we're going to get rid of them forever."

"How forever are you talking about?" Hunter said.

"They'll still be breathing," Miss E. said with a slight smile. "But credibility is never going to be in their corner again."

Hunter chuckled. Leon and his brother didn't know what they'd gotten themselves into when they started tangling with Miss E. They thought she's just a sweet, little old lady who played cards, which was exactly what she wanted most people to think about her. Leon was lost. Miss E. had been a showgirl, a gambler and owned a well-respected poker school. She had more street cred than poor little Leon could ever hope for.

Hunter leaned over and kissed his grandmother on the cheek. "Thank you for being you."

She patted him on the cheek. "I know you don't think purchasing this casino was my brightest idea, but this is going to be a game changer."

"I learned a long time ago to never question what you do too loudly or too long." Even though he thought it a lot.

A loud crack sounded behind them. Hunter whirled to find the scaffolding slowly collapsing to the ground in a series of cracks and pops and thunderous bangs. Someone screamed. Hunter raced toward the scaffolding, trying to see if anyone had been on it, but dust rose to obscure his vision. Miss E. coughed. She dug in her pocket for her phone. More screams and then silence.

The area around the scaffolding was cordoned off. Hunter spoke with the job foreman.

"Thank heaven no one was on it," Hunter said.

Eli Burgess was a big burly man, solidly built with narrow blue eyes and close-cropped brown hair. He wore an orange hard hat that perched on his head like an afterthought. He'd been managing the maintenance department at the hotel for several years and Hunter assumed he knew what he was doing.

Burgess toed at a piece of lumber. "Never had nothing happen like this before." He studied the collapsed scaffolding.

"You don't seem too concerned."

Eli shrugged. "Nobody got hurt."

"But somebody could have." Hunter felt a stirring of anger at the man's nonchalance. "We have a lot of people moving through the lobby all the time. What are you going to do to insure their safety?"

"I'm doing my job, Mr. Russell."

Hunter didn't like this guy. His attitude was a little too casual and blasé. "My job is to make sure things get done on time, as safely as possible. That safety includes both the workers and our patrons."

"Is it possible the scaffolding was not done properly?"

"Are you saying I can't do my job?" Eli looked angry.

"What I'm saying is that things don't always work the way they should no matter how careful you are." Hunter may not like Eli Burgess, but he didn't want to antagonize him.

"I inspected everything as it went up," Eli said. "Nothing was wrong."

"Accidents do happen," Hunter replied. "The next time I inspect every piece of scaffolding with you."

"What do you know?" Burgess demanded.

"I put myself through Berkley working construction." Hunter felt a small moment of satisfaction at the look on Burgess's face.

"Oh," Eli said, disbelief in his eyes.

Hunter could see Burgess didn't think Hunter knew anything about construction. He probably thought Hunter was stupid.

"I don't like people looking over my shoulder. Maybe you better think about getting someone else to run maintenance."

"If you don't like people looking over your shoulder, you must be in the wrong business."

Burgess looked shocked. He shook his head and walked away. After putting distance between him and Hunter, Burgess reached for his cell and was dialing as he walked out the sliding glass doors to the sidewalk beyond. Hunter wondered who Burgess was calling.

Hunter headed toward his office. He needed to talk to Scott and have him keep his eye on this guy. Remembering his brother was meeting with security, he pulled his phone out and texted his brother about the collapse and Burgess's odd behavior. Then he went to his office to wait for the safety inspector.

After the safety inspector left, Hunter went to Lydia's office. He wanted to check on her, but she wasn't there. He took the elevator to her floor and found her sitting on the tile floor of her living room surrounded by paint chips, carpet samples, fabric swatches and photos of spas that looked like she'd taken them off the internet. Maya sipped some sort of punch and sat cross-legged on the sofa punching hearts out of the paint chips and arranging them on a piece of construction paper.

Hunter sat down on the floor with her. "Don't you have an office?"

"I do, but I can't work in it and worry about Maya so I shifted everything up here." She moved paint chips around and tilted her head to look at them from different perspectives.

"So what do you think?" she asked, shoving a paint chip with various shades of gray at him.

"These are nice colors."

"Gray is very sophisticated, I think." She held the chips out at arm's length and squinted her eyes. "But I'd like to see what other spas are doing. With all the different themes at the different hotels, I keep thinking how we're going to stand out."

"Why don't we take a couple of trips to the most popular casinos and hotels and see what they've done."

"I don't want to copy anyone," she said, tilting her head to look at the colors from a different angle.

"Neither do I. We're just going to steal ideas and come up with our own spin."

"I want to see Circus Circus." Maya hopped down from the sofa and showed her mother what she was doing. "One of the girls in my ballet class loves going there to see the circus acts."

"Does Circus Circus have a spa?" Lydia asked.

"I'm sure they do," Hunter replied. All the hotels had spas, but the Mariposa having its own hot springs was a plus.

"I'm a little uncomfortable taking Maya to a casino when Leon and David are being so…" She glanced at her daughter…"over-protective."

What a diplomatic way to put that, Hunter thought. "I don't think you should be too worked up. They have themselves parked at the blackjack tables and if they continue to lose money the way they are, the spa will be paid for in no time at all."

"Maya, why don't you go in your room for a bit so I can talk to Mr. Russell."

"Sure." Maya picked up the paint chips she'd been playing with, along with her staple punch and pad of paper, and walked across the floor to her room.

With Maya gone, Lydia's face took on a worried look. "What's wrong?"

"We had a minor accident a little bit ago. Some scaffolding collapsed."

"Was anyone hurt?" She covered her mouth with her fingers, her eyes concerned.

"No," he said in an emphatic tone, allowing his irritation to come through.

"There's something else?"

"I feel like the collapse wasn't a random accident."

Her beautiful eyes widened. "Why would you think that?"

He didn't want to add to her burden but he wanted to be honest with her. "I don't know, maybe I'm just being paranoid."

"How do you investigate something like this?"

"I'm going to put Scott on it. He's a bloodhound."

She frowned. "What happens if it wasn't an accident?"

"We find out who is behind the collapse and prosecute them to the limit of the law."

She studied him intently. "When you first showed up, I didn't think you were really interested in helping your grandmother."

"I'm allowed to change my mind."

She laughed. "I thought that was only a lady's prerogative."

Hunter grinned at her. She hadn't lost her sense of humor despite having to deal with her stepsons. "And a gentleman always does what a lady wishes." His grandmother had given up a lot to raise Hunter and his siblings. When she should have been doting grandmother, she ended up being a mother for a second term. "My grandmother expected us to conquer the world. We can afford time to help her."

"Not everyone feels that way about their parents, or their grandparents. It's refreshing to see how much you love her."

Hunter moved some fabric samples around. "What about you?"

She thought for a moment. "I love my parents, I really do, but I couldn't wait to get away from them. While the other kids on my street were outside playing, I was taking etiquette lessons or ballroom dancing. When the kids were getting dirty at the playground, I was being taught how to walk properly, to hold my head a certain way and…" Her voice trailed off as she looked backward at the memories.

"Your childhood doesn't sound like there was much fun built into it."

She sighed. "Learning to be a lady takes a lot of time out of a girl's life."

"Maybe it's time you learned to have fun now. Tomorrow we're taking Maya to Circus Circus and having a great time."

Lydia brightened. "Sounds like fun."

"Miss E. used to take us to the one in Vegas all the time. I had tons of fun. So, it's a date."

Lydia clapped her hands. "Good. I'm in need of some serious fun."

"Can fun be considered serious business?"

"Of course it can. I'm going to have to work at it."

There was a little part of him that thought that was sad, but a bigger part of him was glad that he could help her with that too. "We'll go for lunch tomorrow and Maya can spend the afternoon enjoying everything the midway has to offer. And you're going to leave all your worries about Leon and David packed away in a closet and have mindless fun."

"I don't think I've ever had that. You might have to bring instructions."

Hunter shook his head. "Having fun needs no instructions."

She sighed. "I wouldn't be too sure about that. But I do have one rule."

His eyebrows rose. "And that is?"

"No more kisses."

He pulled back slightly. "I don't think I like that rule. I enjoyed our kiss."

"I did, too. I have so much on my plate, I can't balance it all."

"It was just a kiss, Lydia, not a lifetime commitment." The memory of her soft, yielding body so close to his sent a bolt of desire cascading through him. And from the look on her face, she felt it, too. "All right, no kisses tomorrow." He would back off. At least for the moment. But he intended to kiss her again. And maybe again. She was a woman who was meant to be kissed.

"Thank you. My dating experience is very limited. Maybe dating experience isn't the right word."

"We need to rectify that."

"We're not dating," she said hastily as a pretty flush covered her cheeks.

"If you say so." He pushed himself to his feet. "I'll see you tomorrow." He would allow her to think she was in control, but she wasn't.

He left her still sitting on the floor staring at the paint chips scattered among the fabric and carpet samples. How was he going to show her a romantic time with Maya around? What he needed to do was win over Maya. Maya was a great kid, a little lacking in the fun department, but he would take care of that for both of them.

He liked having a plan. He found himself whistling as he headed toward the elevator.

Chapter 5

What did one wear for a casual lunch/casino investigation tour? Lydia had no idea. She stood in front of her closet dressed in a robe, her skin still damp from her shower. She had casual clothes that worked for a casual lunch at a club, but not a circus.

"I don't know what to wear," Lydia said with a sigh.

Maya reached in and pulled out denim jeans and then rummaged through Lydia's dresser drawer and pulled out a blue cotton shirt. "Wear these, Mom. They're comfortable." She dug through the bottom of the closet and pulled out an old pair of flats.

"Yes, but…"

"Mom, you want to be comfortable."

Not too comfortable, Lydia thought. Maya ran to her bedroom to get dressed. Lydia pulled her clothes on and sat on the bed to put on her shoes.

"I like Mr. Hunter," Maya said from the doorway.

Lydia studied her daughter. She liked Hunter, too. "You do. Why?"

"He's nice and doesn't talk to me like I'm three years old."

Lydia tilted her head to look at her daughter. "Who treats you like you're three years old?"

Maya sighed. "Leon and David."

"Sometimes it's hard for grownups to relate to other people's children."

"Leon doesn't like children," Maya said with a wisdom way beyond her years.

Startled, Lydia stared at her daughter. Maya was correct, but Lydia didn't want to let her know she agreed. "How do you know that?"

"Because the only time he and David ever talked to me is when you or Daddy were around and then they asked me stupid stuff. Like do I enjoy playing with dolls. I'm not going to have to live with them, am I?"

"No," Lydia said. "Definitely not." Never. David and Leon might think they had the upper hand, but Lydia knew better.

Maya sighed. "David told me I was going to live with them. I don't want to."

Lydia gathered her daughter into her arms ready to cry. Her heart raced and her anger at the two men grew. They had no right to talk to Maya. "You are not going to have to live with them. Ever."

"Promise?"

Lydia forced back tears. "Promise. Put your shoes on. We're meeting Mr. Hunter in the lobby in ten minutes."

Maya released her and flew out the door and a few minutes later came back with her shoes. She sat on the floor and put them on. "You promise I won't have to live with Leon and David?"

"I solemnly promise." A part of her still worried that they would win their case and she would lose Maya. If it came to that she would take Maya to Europe, where they'd have a harder time trying to get custody. There was no way she'd let Leon and David have her baby.

The elevator was slow to drop. Maya hopped on one foot and looked excited.

"Circus Circus is a casino for kids, right?"

"No, it's more a family friendly casino."

"What does that mean?" Maya asked.

Lydia loved the fact that Maya asked questions. She encouraged her daughter's curiosity. Her own childhood had been more silent. Lydia's parents disliked answering her questions. Her mother's maxim was "children were seen and not heard."

"They have activities for children to do."

"Do they have poker for children? Can I play? Miss E. has been teaching me."

"No, I'm afraid you can't play poker, or gamble. You have to be twenty-one." Amused, Lydia kissed her daughter on the forehead.

"Then why have a family friendly casino?"

"Because the job of a casino is to separate you from your money."

"I have money."

"You're still too young."

"Miss E. and I don't play for money," Maya continued. "We play for M&M's."

Lydia worried that anyone listening to this conversation would question her mothering skills and be inclined to take Maya away from her right then and there. She loved Miss E. and Miss E. was great with Maya. Lydia didn't mind that Miss E. was teaching Maya to play poker, but she was a bit of uncomfortable knowing that Maya wanted to play for money. Did she have budding card shark on her hands?

"Why are we going then?" Maya asked.

"We're going to have some fun and check out the competition. You're going to be my test market."

"What's a test market?"

"When companies decide on a new product, they test it in small areas to a small group of people before selling it to a large group of people. Test marketers are very important."

The elevator stopped at the lobby. The doors slid open.

"So this is like a job. Am I going to get paid?" Maya asked as she dragged Lydia into the lobby. She stopped briefly at the edge of the pond. Several koi rushed toward her. Maya had started feeding them and the fish seemed to recognize her. Maya pulled some pellets out of her pocket and tossed them into the water. The koi raced to grab the food.

"You're going to get fed because food is very important. You can play all the games you want."

Maya giggled. She straightened and glanced at the lobby. "I can't wait. Is it okay if I beat Hunter at the games?"

Lydia stopped and looked at her daughter. "Why would you think that?"

"Because Grandma is always telling me I'm supposed to let boys win because I'm a girl. She said it doesn't matter how much better I am at something."

"No, you're not to let boys win just because you're a girl." Lydia's voice was firm. This was exactly the attitude she hated. She would have to talk to her mother. Lydia wanted Maya to be smart and independent. She didn't want her submissively catering to some man.

Hunter waited for them at the front desk. He wore washed out jeans, a white cowboy shirt open at the neck and boots. Lydia half expected him to pull out a ten gallon hat, but he held a baseball cap instead. Maya skipped up to him.

"Are you going to play games with me today?" Maya asked him, looking up.

"I'll be happy to play games with you." Hunter looked a little confused and Lydia hid a smile.

"Good. I'm not going to let you win because you're a boy and I'm a girl."

Hunter looked curiously at Lydia, who shrugged. "I can live with that."

"My mother insists that when she plays with boys she lets them win so their fragile egos don't become permanently damaged," Lydia explained.

Hunter chuckled. "I'm not going to let her win either."

Oh, great, Lydia thought. "How old are you again? Seven?"

Hunter grinned. "I don't think a man's ego ever gets beyond the age of seven. I read an article recently that said men don't mature until their early forties." He leaned close to Lydia and whispered in her ear. "I was going to let her win, I was just going to make her work for it."

"Just promise me one thing," Lydia whispered back. "Don't do that. She has to earn her victories."

He nodded, respect showing in his eyes. Lydia wasn't used to men respecting her. She took Maya's hand and started toward the doors, uncertain how she felt.

Circus Circus was loud. The café was nicely situated. They had a table overlooking the midway, where they could see people walking back and forth along with a prime view of a juggler, who stood on a small platform and juggled watermelons.

Maya ordered a hamburger and was eating it as quickly as she could, anxious to get to her games.

"Where is she putting it all?" Hunter asked, leaning his elbow on the table.

Lydia sat with her hands in her lap. In her house elbows were not allowed on the table and she couldn't entirely shake off her childhood. "I don't know."

Maya looked up. "In my tummy."

"But you're so skinny. I worry your tummy will burst."

"Nope." Maya shook her head. "I take ballet lessons and I'm going to be taking riding lessons starting tomorrow. Do you see the juggler? I think I want to learn to juggle."

"When will you fit in your schoolwork?"

"Maybe I can stay up until nine-thirty."

"We'll work it out. Slow down, pumpkin," Lydia said. "You'll get an upset stomach."

"But I'm too excited. And you're eating too slow."

Lydia understood that. She had things to do, too. As a child, dinner with her parents had taken forever, with her mother always chastising her to be ladylike, to sit up straight, to chew her food with her mouth closed or other little criticisms. Maya ate fast because she wanted to experience everything she could as fast as she could. Lydia would never dampen her enthusiasm.

Hunter took a huge bite of his hamburger and started chewing.

"Hunter," Lydia said.

He mumbled around the food unintelligibly.

"I can translate that," Maya said. "He says hurry up we have things to do." She popped a french fry into her mouth, giggling.

Lydia laughed. She knew when she was defeated. "What do you want to see?"

Maya pulled a piece of paper out of her pocket. She unfolded the paper. "I want to see the Chinese acrobats, the Russian circus and the trained dogs. We have to hurry; the Chinese acrobats start their show in half an hour."

"We can try to get to all of those, but Hunter and I have other things to check out."

"I know, Mom, but you said you wanted to come here because it's kid friendly. Don't you think we should check out the kid-friendly parts first?" She popped another french fry into her mouth.

"She has a point," Hunter said after a drink from his soda.

She leaned toward Hunter. "Yes, she does have a point, but it's not always good to give in to her even if she has logic on her side."

Hunter raised an eyebrow. "Translation—she keeps you on your toes."

And then some, Lydia thought with a fond look at her precocious daughter. "Exactly."

"Mom," Maya said dramatically. "It's true."

Lydia sighed. She'd wanted a daughter who thought for herself and Maya added her own unique twist to that. "Let's get going if you want to make the acrobat show."

Hunter paid for their lunch and they set off for the theater showcasing the Chinese acrobat show. As they waited in line for the doors to open, Maya's eyes were caught by all the acts that had been staged around the theater. Jugglers, clowns and magicians entertained the crowds of children clustered about them.

Lydia took photos of everything. One thing she noticed was that the casino wasn't nearly as crowded as the entertainment areas. Like Las Vegas, Reno was making itself over as a family friendly entertainment venue. Even Miss E. had commented that the casino areas had been reduced in size to make room for more entertainment.

The Chinese acrobats were marvelous and even Lydia was enchanted with them and their impossible body movements. Maya clapped and screamed. She covered her eyes when the acrobats appeared to do something dangerous and she watched with amazement as they moved.

Afterward, they stood outside the theater trying to decide what to do next.

"I'm hungry," Maya said.

Hunter looked surprised. Lydia simply smiled. "Of course you are."

"How about some ice cream?" Hunter asked.

Maya nodded enthusiastically. They stopped at a small café and sat down at a table. The café was all bold yellow and blue with a ceiling that was painted like a huge tent.

"We're going to have to come back later," Lydia confessed to Hunter once they'd placed their order.

"Yes." Maya clapped her hands.

"Not with you, pumpkin," Lydia said.

"But Circus Circus is for kids."

"That's true," Lydia replied. "Let me explain what I'm thinking. I noticed there are more people in the entertainment areas than in the casinos and I want to know if it's the same after dark when children are in bed. So we need to come back to study that."

"Why?" Hunter asked curiously.

"I know my job is getting the spa built, but I've been thinking about the hotel and casino as a whole. If I were a guest in the Mariposa, I would want everything the hotel has to offer. And as the owner, I want my guests to stay in the hotel, shop, gamble, relax and eat without leaving the premises. We can't compete with the big boys, but we can offer the best of everything. And I want to know what works. Do we need to make the spa a more prominent feature, or the gambling? I want to see what the night life is like in order to figure this out."

"This isn't just a hobby for you, is it?" Hunter asked.

"Do you think I'm just dabbling?"

"Lydia, you can spend the rest of your life doing nothing. And a lot of people, if they were in your shoes, would be doing exactly that."

"I've done that and that is a discussion for when we're

alone." She shot a meaningful glance at her daughter. She wasn't about to tell any details about her marriage in front of Maya. She'd spent her entire marriage going to charity lunches, arranging flowers, shopping and grooming. She was a mom and a wife and she liked being both. What she didn't like were the endless hours left to fill. And when Mitchell and Maya were gone, she had felt a longing to do something more, to accomplish something else.

Her mother would have argued that doing charity work should have been fulfilling enough. Lydia had understood the need for supporting charities, but she wanted something more. She had noticed so many of the women in her social sphere supported charities, not because they believed in them, but because they had something to do to fill the endless hours of their lives.

She sighed. "I have so much to think about, to talk about with your grandmother and Reed. Coming here to Circus Circus has been an eye-opening experience."

"In what way?" Hunter asked.

"Have you noticed that the slot machines here don't even chime anymore? Everything is digital. The Mariposa is so old school."

"Didn't you visit casino before the poker game to see what you were getting into?"

"I'm ashamed to say, I didn't." Lydia dropped her gaze to her plate. "I thought casinos were slot machines, roulette wheels, cocktail waitresses in skimpy little outfits and high stakes poker games."

"They still have skimpy outfits," Hunter said with a chuckle.

"We have to rethink the shopping area. There are shops everywhere here, not grouped together like the Mariposa has them." She gestured with her hand to include the nearest shop, which sold magic tricks. A line of children stood in front of a table watching a woman doing magic tricks with cards.

"And to think this was just supposed to be a fun day with your daughter," Hunter said with a wry smile.

"I'm having a wonderful time." And she was. She enjoyed being with Hunter and Maya. She enjoyed the crowds, the action and the excitement. She enjoyed knowing she was an owner. Every time she thought about the future she saw herself involved with Maya and being Mitchell's dutiful wife, but now she saw a future for herself. Her mother would have told her how selfish she was and a part of her would have believed her.

Thinking about her mother reminded her she needed to call and let her parents know what was happening. She tended to avoid talking to her mother because she was still upset that Lydia had abandoned them for Reno as though she'd shamed the family. Caroline Fairchild was all about visibility and status. For a moment, Lydia wondered about her father, Andrew Fairchild, and how he felt. He'd never voiced his opinion. During her childhood, he had kept his distance from her, always a shadowy figure in the background of her life, who always had a disapproving look on his face. The only time she remembered her father smiling at her was on the day she married Mitchell.

The remainder of the afternoon was spent indulging Maya with her cotton candy obsession, her desire to learn to walk the high wire and how Hunter arranged for her to go backstage and meet all the dogs. That was the moment Lydia knew she would no longer be able to sidestep getting Maya a dog.

By the time they returned to the Mariposa, Maya was half asleep, clutching a stuffed dog she'd chosen from one of the shops because it resembled one of the dogs in the show. Maya looked so happy Lydia could hardly take her eyes off her. She glowed with such contentment, while Lydia soared with her own happiness. She liked being with Hunter. He made everything fun and his attention to Maya made her glow in a way Mitchell had not.

Hunter carried a sleepy Maya into the Mariposa. Cradled in his arms, she looked so small, so vulnerable. Hunter had been sweet to Maya all day. Lydia couldn't help but think what a wonderful father he would make someday. She tried to imagine him with a loving woman against his side and a child clinging to him, but the only vision she had was of her hugged tight against him with Maya holding his hand. She shook her head to banish the vision.

The lobby was in chaos. David and Leon glared at the concierge and hotel manager. Miss E. had one hand out and the other clenched as though she wanted to hit someone.

"I ordered a limo for seven o'clock sharp." Leon looked pointedly at his watch. "It is now five minutes after seven and no limo."

"Sir," the concierge said in a soothing tone, "I have no booking in your name for this time."

"This is an abomination. What kind of sub-par, ramshackle hotel are you running here?" Leon slammed his fist down on the counter. "I get better service from a fast food place."

"Leon," Miss E. said firmly. "We offered you a free ride and a free dinner and you're still upset."

Hunter approached the group, holding Maya tightly in his arms. She opened her eyes drowsily and made some comment he couldn't hear. "What's the problem here?"

Leon turned to glare at Hunter. His gaze took in the sleeping Maya and grew even angrier. "What are you doing with my sister?"

"Just carrying her."

"What kind of man exhausts a child like this?"

Lydia stepped between Hunter and Leon. "Leon, what's going on?"

"This hotel is nothing but a travesty. The food is inedible and pedestrian. The staff is surly and uncooperative. And I think one of your blackjack dealers is cheating me."

Hunter had to think about that statement. For a second he had visions of two bananas walking hand in hand.

"The service," Leon continued, "and staff is shoddy at best. You don't have enough complaint forms for me to fill out…and…"

"Leon," Lydia broke into his rant, "do you really think that by condemning my hotel and casino, you'll win custody of my daughter?"

Maya stirred sleepily in Hunter's arms. Hunter wanted to cover her ears.

"I can't believe you're letting a fine young woman grow up in a place like…" Leon glanced around the lobby, contempt apparent on his face.

"Like what?" Lydia said in a calm tone.

"Like a barbaric, uncouth…" Leon stopped, looking around as though searching for inspiration.

Lydia tilted her head. "You have a lot of nerve calling my casino barbaric and uncouth. I know where your children lived before your father stepped in and found them someplace decent."

"Don't you bring my children into this."

"Really? You're willing to question me about how I'm raising my daughter. I think I'm being more than fair when I question how you are raising your children. You have an offer for a free limo and free dinner on the hotel. I'll be happy to help you pack up your things and arrange for you to stay in another hotel. Or take you to the airport."

"We do have the right to refuse service to people,"

Hunter said calmly. Maya had woken up and struggled to be put down, her eyes wide as she took in the scene being played out in front of her. Hunter wanted to shield her, but too much had already been said.

An elevator door opened and Scott exited. He glanced around and then made his way to Hunter. "I was informed there's a disturbance."

Miss E. glared at Leon. "Just a minor one." She quickly explained the problem to Scott.

Scott looked Leon and David up and down. "Gentlemen, either we take this conversation to my office, or we go outside. Either one is good for me."

Leon glared. "Are you threatening me and my brother?"

"No, I'm just offering to help you take your bags to your car and be on your merry way." Scott cracked his knuckles.

Leon wet his lips nervously, his gaze darting back and forth.

"What's your decision?" Scott asked, leaning against the concierge's desk.

Hunter tried not to smile. Scott being intimidating always made him want to laugh.

Lydia looked shocked, but Miss E. smiled proudly with her "that's my boy" look on her face.

Leon stuttered. David shrugged, always the follower. "We'll take the limo and the dinner." With a hand around his brother's arm, David pulled Leon out the door.

"This isn't over, Lydia," Leon said before the doors slid open to the cool desert evening.

Lydia hugged Maya to her. "Okay, Leon. If you say so." Her tone was tired and dispirited. "This is really going to get ugly, isn't it?" She pulled Maya to her and hugged her tightly.

"Momma, what's wrong?" Maya asked. "Why are you fighting with Leon and David?"

"David and Leon are just unhappy right now." Lydia ran a hand through her hair.

"I don't like Leon and David anymore," Maya said firmly. "And they don't like me."

Hunter could see anxiety in Lydia's eyes and sense her every fear. He squatted down in front of Maya. "Don't worry, sweetie. The adults will make everything right."

Maya didn't look comforted. She gazed up at her mother.

Miss E. held out her hand to Maya. "Come on, kiddo. Why don't we go upstairs and get you ready for bed. Your mom and Hunter need to talk."

Maya took Miss E.'s hand and let her guide her to the elevator. She glanced back at Lydia once before allowing herself to be distracted by Miss E.'s infectious laughter.

Hunter watched the tension leave Lydia the moment she sat down on the rock, pulled off her shoes and dangled her feet in the hot springs. She pulled her hair loose and fluffed it around her shoulders.

"I hate having my daughter be the center of all this un-needed drama."

Hunter sat next to her. He wanted to comfort her as much as he wanted to comfort Maya. "You didn't start this fight, but you need to end it. And I'm telling you that those two idiots have pissed off the wrong people."

"Are you going to be bad cop?"

Hunter shook his head, grinning. "I'm the nice one. Scott, on the other hand, was very well paid to be mean, nasty and underhanded, and he was very good at what he did."

"He's not going to do anything to hurt them?" Lydia stared at the moon rising over the desert.

"You don't want to know."

Lydia leaned against him and he slid an arm around her. She sighed in contentment. "I wish they would just go away and leave me in peace."

"You're going to have to make them go away," Hunter said. The world was full of Leons and Davids who felt the world not only belonged to them, but they could order it to their satisfaction.

"If their worry is just about money, I'm happy to share."

"They are not going to go away. No matter how much money you give them, they'll run through it and come back for more. If your husband had wanted them to have money, he would he would have given it to them. Don't shortchange Maya."

She splashed her toes in the warm water. Behind them, the lights in the pool area started to go off as the people began shutting the pool and adjacent cabanas down for the night.

"Maya doesn't need six hundred fifty million dollars," Lydia said quietly.

"Neither do David and Leon."

She glanced up at him. "You're not helping."

"I hate bullies and I specifically hate bullies who try to leverage a child to get what they want. The worst thing you can do is give in to them."

"There you are," Scott said as he walked down the pathway.

"What's wrong?" Lydia asked, tensing up again. "Is Maya all right?"

"Maya's fine, but you need to come to the lobby right now."

What new drama awaited them? Hunter thought as Lydia slipped her wet feet back into her sandals. He pulled on his socks and shoes and followed her into the hotel.

Lydia strode purposefully through the long winding

corridors to the lobby, where she stopped so suddenly Hunter ran into her.

A tall, imposing man with graying hair stood at the desk. He wore an excellently tailored suit and power tie. Next to him stood a small, slender woman dressed in a beautifully shaped dress that hugged her small, slender figure to perfection. From Lydia's resemblance to them, Hunter knew immediately these were Lydia's parents, Andrew and Caroline Fairchild. He almost chuckled. Somehow, he'd been expecting them to show up, too.

"Mother," Lydia said in confused tone. "Father. What are you doing here?"

Her father gazed at her. "Lydia, my God, what have you gotten yourself into?"

Chapter 6

Lydia pressed her mouth together tightly to keep her angry retort inside. She started to think of something that would placate them, but couldn't form those words either. She was twenty-nine years old and refused to be treated like a child any longer. Standing up to her parents wasn't easy, but if she wanted a life out from under their thumbs, she knew she needed to find the steel inside her Miss E. insisted she had.

Her father approached her with firm steps, his face set in lines of authority. "Lydia," he said in a quiet tone, "if only you'd come to me for advice. I would have talked you out of this…this…poorly conceived adventure."

Caroline looked at Lydia with sadness in her eyes. "Everyone in New Orleans is so concerned that you've abandoned your senses after Mitchell's passing. Now that we're here we'll fix this, we'll find a way to extricate you from this dreadful situation you've gotten yourself into."

Lydia felt irritation rising. "Fix what? Do you know anything about painting a wall, or plumbing?"

"Don't talk back to your mother," Andrew Fairchild said in a commanding tone.

Patience, Lydia told herself. She pasted a smile on her face. "We need to get you a room and then we can discuss all your concerns in the morning."

"You are not brushing us off," her father said.

"Well, if you want to sit here and talk, that's okay. I've had a long day and I'm going to bed. I'll see you in the morning for breakfast at seven o'clock. We can talk then."

"You know I never wake up before ten, Lydia," her mother admonished her.

"Unfortunately, on this side of the country, things start early. I have a daughter and I have a job. You will have to accommodate me."

Caroline looked shocked and her father frowned. "No self-respecting Fairmont woman has ever needed a job."

"I didn't need a job, I just wanted one."

Her mother stared at her, eyes wide. Her father's frown deepened. Lydia turned to the reception desk and requested a small suite on the third floor for her parents, thinking to keep them as far away from her as she could get them. The desk clerk smiled happily and assigned a suite. She could just imagine her parents looking at the western decor in their room and thinking how awful it was. Maybe they would leave then. Lydia didn't want them here. She refused to be put back in the box her father demanded she live in.

Lydia handed them their keys and she headed toward the elevator.

"Aren't you going to show us to our room?" Andrew asked.

"That's what bellhops are for." If Lydia were mean she wouldn't have offered a bellhop, but she knew her parents probably already had one since they seldom traveled with less than a dozen suitcases.

Hunter stepped forward. He held his hand out to Andrew.

"Who are you?" Andrew asked.

"I'm the man who's trying to put this place back together."

Caroline's eyebrows shot up. "You're the hired help?"

Hunter paused. "Not exactly."

"Other than being the grandson of one of the owners, I'm an architect and I'll be redesigning the hotel."

At last her parents had the dignity to look embarrassed. She wanted to enjoy their discomfort, but that would be wrong. She glanced at Hunter and silently mouthed the words *thank you*. He grinned back at her. She could see he enjoyed baiting her parents. She wished she'd learned that skill much earlier in life.

"Where is Maya?" Caroline asked. "I want to see for myself that she is adjusting well to the upheaval you've caused in her life."

"Maya is fine. Now if you'll excuse me, I'm going to bed." She turned on her heel and left, knowing her parents would probably be angry at her abrupt departure, but she'd already had enough drama for the day.

Hunter held the elevator for Caroline and Andrew. He was proud of Lydia. She'd stood up to them and didn't cave no matter how her father tried to intimidate her. Caroline entered, giving him a curious glance. Andrew brushed past him and stood in the center of the elevator waiting for Hunter to push the button.

"Lydia has never worked a day in her life," Andrew said.

"I wouldn't have known that considering how hard she works now."

"I didn't raise my daughter to be a drone worker bee," Andrew replied.

Hunter smiled. "She's not. She has no problem telling people what to do, what she likes and how she likes having things done."

"Andrew," Caroline said in a placating tone, "maybe

she just needs a little independence and to discover it's not as glamorous as she thinks, and then she'll come home."

Hunter eyed the woman. Did she believe that? He thought about saying something, but decided to let them keep thinking that Lydia was just having an adventure. Their baby girl was not going back to the mansion anytime ever. She was never going back. She'd have to fall on her cute little butt, crawl through the mud and get run over by a train before she'd even think about going back. He wasn't going to say anything to them while he was trapped in an elevator with them. Things could get ugly.

The elevator door opened to a long hallway. Hunter led them out of the foyer and down the corridor.

"She'll be back," Andrew said. "She knows her proper place in the world."

Hunter was amazed at what they were saying and realized they didn't consider him a person of any consequence. Not being on their radar didn't bother him at all.

"At least," Caroline said, "she's doing it here instead of New Orleans, where we would have to bear the shame of it."

Wow, Hunter thought as he led them down the corridor toward their suite. Her parents were the most insensitive, callous people he'd ever meet. He wanted to help Lydia more. He wanted her to succeed just to spite them. How did someone as sweet and nice as Lydia come from them? If she didn't look exactly like her mother, he'd think she was adopted.

He opened the door to their suite and stood politely aside to let them inside. Caroline stood just inside the door, her gaze moving from one corner to the next, her gaze critical as she took in the too fussy decor. "I expected something...well, better."

"We're working on that," Hunter said, making no move to elaborate.

"How do I make an appointment at the spa?" Caroline walked into the suite.

"We don't have a spa, but we do have an arrangement with a spa a few blocks from here. I'll be happy to make an appointment."

Caroline turned shocked eyes on him. "What kind of luxury hotel do you have without a spa?"

"We are hotel in transition, Mrs. Fairchild. And had we known you would be arriving, we would have had everything in place for you." Hunter tried not to sound condescending. These two people just rubbed him the wrong way. "All I can do is ask for your forgiveness and understanding."

Caroline sniffed scornfully and headed toward the bedroom. Hunter knew when he'd been dismissed even though he thought he'd gotten the upper hand with them.

Lydia waited for her parents in the café. Maya was with her tutor, who'd agreed to come earlier to fit in her lessons before her horse-back riding lesson.

Her father was late. She glanced at her watch, trying to decide how long she should wait for him. She had work to do and his deliberate little ploy annoyed her. He wanted to make sure she knew he was in charge. She'd give him five more minutes.

She finished her coffee and just as she rose, her father entered the café, looking overdressed for the more casual atmosphere.

"Lydia," Andrew said.

"I was just about to leave," Lydia said. "So you have five minutes." She glanced pointedly at her watch.

He sat across from her. "What do you mean I have five minutes?"

"I have a meeting with Miss E. in a few minutes. You're twenty minutes late."

"I'm your father; you do not speak to me in that tone of voice."

"And I'm a businesswoman with a company to run," Lydia retorted.

His eyebrows rose. "What do you know about running a business?"

"I know enough to show up to a meeting on time. You're wasting your five minutes arguing with me." She leaned back and crossed her arms over her chest. "I'm waiting."

Her father stared at her, his lips twitching and one hand gripping his mug of coffee. For a second she felt five years old again and afraid of her parents. She thrust her chin forward; she wasn't about to let him know her fear.

"Very well," her father said in a short, clipped tone. "Your mother and I feel you need to come home to New Orleans. Should you refuse to, I will support the custody battle in favor of Leon and David."

Lydia went very still, trying to wrap her mind around her father's words. She shouldn't be shocked that her parents sided with her stepsons. She'd had three months of perspective and had figured out that her parents were notorious in getting their way when they wanted it. She'd watched her father manipulate and scheme. Hurt filled her, but she wasn't surprised.

"I see." She slid out of the booth, stood and braced her hands against the table. Her father's face was guarded, as though he'd figured he'd gone too far.

Lydia straightened, her back stiff, resolved to fight a battle her parents would never forget. She whirled on her heels and walked away.

"Lydia, come back here, I'm not finished."

"I am," she muttered to herself as she left the café and headed to Miss E.'s office.

Once in Miss E.'s office, she sat at the conference table, trying to calm herself. In her whole life she couldn't remember being so angry. Her parents siding with her stepsons made her want to do something criminal.

The door opened and Miss E. entered. With one look at Lydia's face, Miss E. sat down and asked quietly, "What happened?"

Lydia wanted to cry. All her life she worked hard at not shaming her family and here they were threatening to air their dirty laundry and embarrass everyone. Mitchell spent a lot of time and money keeping Leon's and David's skeletons firmly in the closet. Her parents' betrayal hurt more than anything.

The words seemed to explode out of her. "My loving parents decided to support any claim David and Leon have in taking Maya away from me."

"What?"

"They think my stepsons would be better parents for Maya than I would. Unless I return to New Orleans, my parents will support them." Even saying the words made her angry.

"Well," Miss E. said in a composed tone. "This fight has just gotten interesting. The gloves are off. I'm rather excited."

"How can you be excited? Am I supposed to be excited?" Mitchell had spent years cultivating his gentlemanly reputation and his sons wanted to destroy it because of their greed and anger. Leon and David were being cruel and selfish, two things she didn't want Maya to be. No matter how she shielded Maya, she was going to end up damaged in some way.

"Do you know what courage is, dear?"

Lydia tried to smile, but her lips refused. "I have an idea, but I'll let you tell me."

"Courage is when you're afraid and you jump into the battle anyway."

Lydia looked down at her hands, clasped so tightly her fingers dug painfully into her palms. "David and Leon, I understand. It's all about the money. But my parents supporting them, I don't understand." They were being cruel and selfish, too. They weren't putting Maya's welfare first. How could they be that way to their own grandchild?

"They probably just want you back home in New Orleans," Miss E. said.

"The last three months have been the most freedom I've ever had in my whole life. And I think that's the real problem. My father can't control me anymore, which is interesting because he didn't try to control me while Mitchell was alive."

"Because Mitchell was doing all the controlling," Miss E. said. "Why did you marry him?"

"I was afraid of disappointing my parents. Mitchell offered me a way out of that house. I thought I would be independent, but looking back I know Mitchell chose me because of how my parents made me. I loved him."

Miss E. nodded. "Did you? Really?"

"I loved him because he gave me Maya." She could have managed anything as long as she had Maya. "He loved her, too. Though at the time, it seemed a different type of love than he had for David and Leon. I could never quite figure out why."

She fell silent thinking, wondering. She married Mitchell because her parents had talked her into it. "Why am

I such a threat to my parents?" In a way, she knew. Her striking out on her own was a repudiation of who she was, who her parents were and their position in the social strata they'd created for themselves.

"Threat may not be the word. You're not threatening them. You're undermining what they see as their 'authority.'" Miss E. put quote marks with her fingers around the word *authority.* "I'm sure they love you. I would even go so far as to think, in their minds, they think they are doing what is best for you."

Lydia rubbed her eyes. She was twenty-nine years old and knew what was best for her and her daughter. Being smothered by her parents' affection wasn't it. She needed to start living her own life. Making decisions was the first step.

"So what do I do?" Lydia asked Miss E.

"I think the first thing we need to do is find out why your parents are supporting David and Leon."

"How do we find this out?"

Miss E. smiled. "Do what I always do. Follow the money."

"Is everything about money?"

Miss E. nodded. "It's about what money represents, what it can do. Money can make an ugly man sexy and a mean woman tolerable. Money can buy love, comfort, safety, revenge. Money can't buy happiness, but it can make being miserable more comfortable."

Lydia digested Miss E.'s words. "I've never thought about money that way."

"You've never had to live from paycheck to paycheck. Knowing that if you can't bluff you opponent looking to fill an inside straight, your babies aren't going to eat."

"Are you telling me, Miss E., it's all about the bluff?"

"You can count cards until the cows come home and

you can read people, but unless you know how to bluff, you won't get anywhere."

"Do you think my parents are bluffing?" Lydia frowned.

Miss E. tilted her head. "I'll know when I meet them."

She found herself telling Miss E. about her meeting with her dad.

"Lydia, brilliant. I'm quite proud of you."

"Thank you, I needed that." Lydia's smile trembled slightly, but she felt better.

"Keep in mind, I'm in your corner. You are not alone."

"I'm scared," Lydia admitted.

"I would expect no less of you." Miss E. took a deep breath. "I almost lost my grandchildren. Someone called Child Services and complained that I was endangering my grandchildren with my lifestyle. The social worker who came to check on me was not a native. She said my being a professional gambler put the children at risk, until I showed her all the professional gamblers with children. They were all white men and the real problem was that I was a single black woman. Single mothers could be waitresses, strippers or prostitutes in Pahrump, but I couldn't be a professional gambler and be a mother. In the social worker's world, black women couldn't be professional gamblers."

"You're entire life rested on the turn of a card."

Miss E. shook her head. "I put money away and I never played for more than I could afford to lose. If I lost it, I stopped for the day, or week, or month."

"How much money did you make?"

"My goal was a thousand dollars a day. And I gambled five days a week."

"You gambled five thousand dollars a week?"

Miss E. nodded. "I had a cushion. There were days I didn't bring home that much money and there were days when I brought double that amount. But most of the time,

I brought home exactly a thousand dollars. The nice thing about Vegas was that I could send the kids to school, gamble until school let out and arrive back home in time to clean the house, greet them at the door and put dinner on the table. I was successful because I treated it like a job. To me it was no different than working as a waitress or a clerk in a department store. And when each of my grandchildren went off to college, I had the money to pay for it. I owned my home, I had a respectable savings account and investments and I never let it go to my head. And there were a lot of other gamblers there just like me. They treated it like a job."

Lydia sighed. "I wish you'd been my mother." Her mother had made a lot compromises to keep her marriage on an even keel. Her father was not an easy man to live with. Caroline wanted everything to be perfect. She created a perfect marriage and a perfect daughter. Looking back, Lydia knew her mother had had no life beyond what her father needed. And that is what Lydia did for Mitchell.

"No, dear, you don't. I was not a fun parent."

"Neither was mine."

"I was exceptionally loving and supportive." Miss E. smiled sweetly. "My kids know how to play poker. And you're going to win. You're going to bluff your parents to lay down their hand."

"From the first time since Leon and David arrived, I feel like I can do this."

"Of course, you can. You have something your parents, David and Leon don't have. You have me, Hunter, Scott and Reed, and in the next few weeks, you will have the rest of my grandchildren in your corner. The Russells travel in packs. Now, we need to get back to business. You need to be incredibly successful if for no other reason than to spite Leon and David and show your parents you're not an ornament, but a woman in charge of her own destiny."

Miss E. opened a file folder in front of her and started talking about Hunter's ideas for the spa. Lydia took a deep breath, calming her nerves. She turned her mind to what Miss E. was saying, putting her problems at the back of her mind to think about later.

A knock sounded on the door frame of his office. Hunter looked up to find Lydia standing there, a booklet in one hand. He had already heard about her interview with her father from Miss E. A hearty dislike for the man grew inside him. How could any father hurt his daughter so much?

"I've been thinking," she said. "I need to buy a house." She waved the booklet with the title Real Estate in Reno on the cover.

"Okay," he replied. His heart did a little lurch. He wasn't certain how he felt about her leaving. He liked having her down the hall from him.

"I want you to help me. I've never bought a house before." She sat down and opened the booklet across her lap. "You're an architect. You know what I should look for."

"What do you want?"

"Privacy, security, a place to keep a horse, good school district." She handed him the booklet. "Like this one. It's on ten acres, completely fenced, generous sized house with a pool and comes with a barn and corral."

Hunter glanced at the photos. "This is what you get for four millions dollars in Reno. In San Francisco, four million would buy you a shack. You know once she sees that barn, she's going to want a horse to put in it."

"In my head I'm preparing for that."

He needed to choose his words with care. "Riding is

dirty and hot and outside. You don't seem like the outdoors type."

She lifted her chin. "I can be any type I want to be."

"I didn't mean to insult you," he said quickly.

"I'm not insulted," she said in a small voice. "I need to
get Maya out of this hotel and into a proper home. I want
to get a big dog and a cat and maybe a rabbit. I want Maya
to have the childhood I never had. I want her to get dirty."

"Okay, let's go take a look at it." He pushed out from
his desk.

"But…but…right this minute?"

"Why not? Do you have someplace you need to be?"

She shook her head.

"Neither do I. Let's go. I can eyeball a house and in
ten minutes and tell you everything that's right or wrong
with it. People pay me big bucks to do this. Don't tell my
grandmother I'm doing it for free." He pushed back from
his desk and grinned at her.

She grinned at him. "Your secret is safe with me."

Chapter 7

The house Lydia had chosen from the real estate guide had already sold. The realtor escorted her and Hunter to a different property.

On the outside, the estate looked perfect. The house was large and rambling, with two wings spreading out from a central entryway. The living area was to the right and the bedrooms were to the left. Between the wings there was a large pool. Outbuildings consisted of a pool house, a guesthouse, a stable with attached corrals and a craft house all spread out over ten acres. She wasn't certain what a craft house was, though figured she would eventually find out.

The Realtor was a sprightly woman in her sixties, smartly dressed in a dark blue pant suit. Her silver white hair was swept up into a neat twist secured with a couple of jeweled pins. Her nametag read Margaret Sorenson.

Lydia wandered around the kitchen, smiling at the professional appliances. She didn't know how to cook, but that was her list of things to learn. A small thrill coursed through her. Yes, this was almost perfect. She could imagine Maya running through the house, her footsteps echoing on the wood floors. She could see a roaring fire in the fireplace. She even could imagine Hunter sitting in the family room with his feet up on a hassock...Lydia shied away from going further.

She liked Hunter. She liked him a little too much and she was confused because she didn't want to like him.

"Sir," the Realtor said to Hunter, "this is a professional chef's kitchen. I can see your wife is quite taken with it."

Lydia looked up and Hunter grinned back at her. She felt all tingly inside over the Realtor's mistake. She didn't correct Margaret and neither did Hunter. Lydia had originally planned to stay in the hotel for a year or two, but knew having a permanent home would work in her favor.

"How many children do you have?" Margaret inquired, but instead of waiting for an answered rushed on. "There are four bedrooms, plenty of space for kids. If you like to barbecue, you'll enjoy the outdoor kitchen, which you can see from here." She pointed out the window. "There is a stable with stalls for eight horses and two attached corrals. The man who owned this place before was what we call a gentleman rancher. He raised quarter horses. Several of your neighbors raise show horses and jumpers. Very social was Mr. Carpenter. He liked to entertain." Margaret chattered on and on.

Lydia knew that if Hunter didn't have anything bad to say about this house, she was ready to plunk down the three point nine million in a second. But she needed to return with Maya.

"The school district is excellent," Margaret said.

Lydia's shoes clicked on the wood floor. She opened a door to find a powder room. Another door proved to be a large linen closet and a third door opened to a small pantry with floor-to-ceiling shelves.

"Mr. Carpenter had what he called a craft house with an exercise room, an office and a wood shop. Mr. Carpenter's son was into wood-crafting. He's quite well-known for his birds. Creates them with a chain saw. The guesthouse has two bedrooms. The pool house has four showers and two changing rooms."

Lydia stopped listening. She'd left the kitchen behind for the dining room. Since no one lived in the house except a security guard who was staying in the guesthouse, she felt she could explore freely without bursting in on the family hidden somewhere to stay out of the Realtor's way. Lydia resented the fact that she would have to find a place for her bodyguard to stay if things continued with Leon and David. Mays should be able to live in a house and be safe from her own brothers. That thought put a taint on the excitement of her house-hunting adventure.

As she wandered she could hear the Realtor giving Hunter her spiel. His sharp eyes would note any problems and she could trust him. She wanted to bring Maya back as quickly as possible. She wanted Maya to feel as empowered as she was feeling. She hugged herself, thrilled to be buying her own house under her name.

Later, Hunter drove around the neighborhood checking out who else lived on the quiet lane and where the shopping and schools were.

"Did you find anything wrong with the house?" Lydia asked. "I loved it and I want Maya to love it."

"The house was last renovated in 2005. And other than some cosmetic things, it's in pretty good shape. I like that it's completely fenced since one of the things I look at is security."

"Then I'm bringing Maya back to look it over."

"Are you sure you don't want to look at a few more houses?"

"No."

Hunter chuckled. "But what happens if Maya doesn't like it?"

"I could be looking at a shack, but as long as it has a

stable, Maya will love it because it means she's getting her horse."

"Do you want me to help you with the negotiation?"

Lydia thought for a moment. "No." She was going to do this on her own. From now on she would live her own life, make her own mistakes and then fix them. She was no longer Mitchell's wife, or Andrew and Caroline's daughter. She was Lydia Fairchild Montgomery.

Lydia opened the door to the suite and found her mother sitting on the sofa while Maya walked back and forth.

"Walk a little more slowly and hold your head like this." Caroline struck a pose and Maya tried to imitate it.

"What are you doing?" Lydia asked.

"Maya runs around like a heathen half the time and I'm showing her how to be a lady." The look on Caroline's face expressed that she considered Lydia lacking in appropriate mother behavior. That was all the more reason to get Maya out of the hotel and out of the clutches of all these people who considered her daughter nothing but a commodity.

Lydia kissed her daughter on the cheek. "Would you go to your room, please? Grandma and I have to have a talk."

Maya took off with a small whoop. Lydia turned to her mother, trying to keep the anger out of her voice. "Maya is my daughter, mother."

"I know, darling," her mother replied calmly. "But I don't feel you are imparting the correct values to my granddaughter."

"And you think Leon and David will impart the proper values to her."

"They'll have her in New Orleans and I've agreed to help them."

"Her home is with me," Lydia said firmly. She studied the woman poised so carefully on the sofa. Her face was smooth and still beautiful, without one wrinkle. No one would guess Caroline was almost fifty-two. She looked twenty years younger. Lydia could never remember ever really seeing any emotion. Caroline had always told Lydia that smiling or frowning caused wrinkles. She gave tiny grins at times, but little else. Her figure was perfect despite seldom exercising. On the surface she was flawless. When Lydia had been in high school, she'd wondered what her mother felt beneath the surface.

"A hotel is not a home," Caroline said.

"Things are about to change," Lydia said. "As soon as I take Maya to look at it, and she approves, I'm buying a house."

"So that's where you've been all day," her mother said, a small frown marring her flawless skin. "You should have spoken to your father first."

"Why? Do you think I'm incapable of purchasing a house?"

"You're not staying in Reno. There's no reason to buy a home."

"I'm beginning a new life and that new life isn't going to be in New Orleans."

"But you have to come home, Lydia." Panic welled in Caroline's eyes. "You've had your great big adventure and now it's time to come home and settle down."

Lydia bit the inside of her lip. So many responses came to her, most of them inappropriate. Lydia tilted her head to study her mother. She loved this woman, but she didn't like her. "I married Mitchell and had Maya. How more settled should I have been?"

Caroline's face suddenly twisted with agony, and tears leaked out of her eyes. "Please, Lydia. Just come home to New Orleans. If you do, David and Leon will drop their suit."

Lydia leaned forward. "Mom, Leon and David aren't going to drop their suit. You know they aren't. I just don't understand why now. Mitchell's been gone for two years."

Caroline sniffed delicately. Even when she cried she was still beautiful. Lydia handed her a handkerchief. Her mother opened her mouth and closed it. Opened it again, then crushed the handkerchief against her mouth, jumped to her feet and ran out the front door.

Lydia stared after her mother in surprise. What the hell had just happened?

The late afternoon heat had given way to cooler early evening shadows.

"What do you think?" Lydia asked her daughter. The Realtor had unlocked the front door and gone to wait in her car while Lydia showed the property to Maya. Maya allowed Lydia to lead her through the house, but not until they reached a bedroom Lydia announced could be hers did she start jumping up and down. "Would you really buy this house so I can have a horse?"

"I want to buy this house because I feel comfortable here and I want you to feel comfortable, too, and part of that feeling is you having a horse." Lydia watched the play of emotions cross her daughter's face.

"Can I have a purple bedroom?" Maya asked hopefully.

"If you can live with a purple bedroom for the next few years, I'll see what I can do." A purple bedroom! Lydia tried not to shudder.

Maya raced across the floor and threw her arms around Lydia's waist. "Thank you, Mom. I'm so excited. Can I have a dog, too?"

"One pet at a time, dear. One pet at a time." Lydia hugged her daughter back.

Lydia loved the look of excitement in Maya as they explored first the house and then the surrounding structure. Lydia had never felt this kind of excitement as a child. Her mother had considered such flagrant emotion as unseemly. A lady was sedate and self-contained, controlling her emotions at all times. Maya's happiness was contagious.

When Lydia and Maya finished the tour, the Realtor locked up the house again and left them.

Lydia turned onto the main road.

"Mom, what are they doing?"

Lydia glanced at the fenced area Maya pointed to. A group of young girls mounted on horses raced back and forth around three white-and-orange-striped barrels. The girls wore Western garb, Stetson type hats firmly on their heads.

Lydia parked on the side of the road so Maya could watch. Maya pressed her nose against the window and watched, bouncing a little in excitement.

"I think they're barrel racing, though I'm not sure."

"I like that. That's what I want to learn," Maya said.

"You want to be a rodeo rider?"

"That's so awesome," Maya cried.

Lydia pictured Maya doing show jumping and dressage. She could see Maya on her horse looking all elegant and refined in white pants, black boots and black jacket. Lydia's mind stuttered to a halt. Oh…my…God, she thought. She was thinking like her mother.

Maya opened the car door and jumped out of the car. She waved frantically at the girls. Lydia followed her quickly.

One of the girls trotted to the fence. She looked about ten years old, with pretty freckles dotting her cream-colored skin and reddish brown hair secured into two braids.

"Hi, I'm Maya and my mom is buying that house over there." Maya pointed.

"Hi, neighbor. I'm Patti Ibarra."

Maya climbed the fence until she was even with the horse's head. "My mom says you're barrel racing. Are you?"

"We're practicing our barrel racing."

Maya leaned over the top rail. "That sounds like so much fun. How do I learn?"

The girl grinned. "My dad teaches us. We compete at the junior rodeos. There's one tomorrow night at the fairgrounds if you want to come."

"Wow, I want to go. Can he teach me?"

"He can teach anybody," Patti said.

Her horse nibbled at the tips of Maya's hair and she patted the soft nose.

"Can he teach my mom, too?"

"No, no," Lydia said, "I want to watch you do this." Lydia couldn't see herself racing around barrels. In fact, it looked a little dangerous. But then again, how dangerous could it be. These girls were barely older than Maya.

"Come on, Mom. It looks like fun. You said you wanted to try new things."

"Watching you learn to barrel race is a new thing," Lydia said. Up close and personal to the horse, Lydia was aware of how large it was. Patti looked so tiny on top the broad back.

Maya gave her a skeptical look. Lydia was sticking with that answer.

"Mom," Maya cried.

Lydia smiled at Patti. "We'll be in touch."

Lydia herded Maya back into the car. "Are you sure you don't want to learn show jumping? It's so beautiful and elegant."

"Did you see the way those horses moved? They were like cheetahs." Maya secured her seat belt.

Lydia maneuvered the car back onto the road and

headed back to the hotel. As frightened as she was about striking out on her own, Lydia knew she wasn't going back to the stifling atmosphere of New Orleans. She was also proud of Maya for showing her independence. Lydia would never have told her mother what she wanted to do. If Maya wanted to barrel race, Lydia was going to let her do it.

Hunter sat at his desk trying to find inspiration. As a historical restorations expert, he worked with buildings already built. He hadn't designed a building from the ground up in a good long while. He wanted to get this one right, because he wanted to impress Lydia.

With pencil poised over a notebook, he started a list of what a woman would want in a spa. As he scribbled down each idea, the overall shape of the building began to grow in his mind.

The door to his office banged with impatient knocks.

"Come in," he called.

Maya bounced in, followed more sedately by Lydia.

Maya was talking a mile a minute. Hunter tried to follow the barrage of words but all he could make out were rodeo, horse, barrel racing and purple cowboy boots. He glanced at Lydia, eyebrows raised.

She mouthed the words "I know" and shrugged.

Maya stopped talking to take a breath. "I want to go to the rodeo. There's one tomorrow night and we should go. It would be fun."

"Rodeo!" Again he looked at Lydia.

"Tomorrow night at the fairgrounds. It's a junior rodeo."

"And I want to be a junior rodeo-ette," Maya announced. "And do barrel racing."

Hunter found himself grinning. Her delight was infectious. "I've never been to one. I think a rodeo would be fun."

"I've never been either." Lydia wasn't certain she really wanted to go to the rodeo, but the idea did sound enjoyable.

"We'll go tomorrow night," Hunter said.

"You'll meet my new friend, Patti." Maya skipped to the door. "I have to tell Miss E. all about it."

Hunter picked up his phone and began dialing, "Hang on, there, half pint." Scott answered and Hunter explained that Maya was looking for Miss E. and requested an escort. He hung up and ten seconds later, Scott opened the door and walked in. "Need a ride?" he asked Maya.

Maya giggled. "Miss E., please."

Scott held out a hand and she slid her fingers into his.

After Scott left with Maya in tow, Hunter said, "The rodeo!"

"I know," Lydia said with a sigh. "I had something more in mind for her, like show jumping with those beautiful costumes and prancing horses and…" She stopped. "I wanted to tell Maya no way, this is not happening, but then I heard my mother's voice in my head and realized I was sounding just like her."

"Would it help any if I told you I think you made the right decision?"

"Yes, because God forbid she be twenty-nine years old and realizing she's just made her first independent decision."

Hunter pushed back from the desk and stood. He put his arms around Lydia and she leaned her head against his chest. "Motherhood is not for sissies."

"No, it isn't."

"I don't care what Leon and David say. You're a great mom."

"Thank you. Speaking of Leon and David," Lydia said, slipping out of his arms and putting a little bit of distance between them. "Have they done anything I should know about?"

"Just general skulking." Hunter stifled a laugh. "Apparently, Leon and David, who treat the staff like dirt, have been offering them money to find out dirt about you."

"What is the staff saying?" Lydia felt her heart thud rapidly in her chest.

"First off, they all think you're a great boss. Secondly, they all think you're a great mother. I haven't found anyone who dislikes Maya."

"So the staff is playing both sides of the fence. Good for them."

"I'm kind of surprised," he said.

"Why?"

"They're gossiping about you and you project a certain image." Hunter didn't like the fact that Leon and David were paying for gossip.

Lydia smiled. "There's nothing to gossip about me. Every penny the staff can take from those reprehensible, rude, conniving men, good for them. Just as long they tell the truth, I'm fine."

"Miss E. would kick them out if she knew." Hunter frowned. His grandmother hated gossip.

"No, she wouldn't. She would let them stay as long as they wanted, just so she could keep an eye on them."

"My grandmother knows how to play the game," he said with a sigh. "Have you had dinner yet?"

"No."

"Let's head over to the lounge. They have jambalaya on the menu tonight and want your opinion."

"Then let's go. Let me check with Miss E., and see if she can watch Maya for a few hours."

A thrill radiated through her. She wanted to have dinner with him. She lifted the phone to her ear to talk to Miss E.

as she walked down the hallway. She thought about how her life was changing, becoming more than what she'd ever dreamed of. She wanted Hunter in her life, yet the idea was still nerve-wracking. Making the decision was one thing, implementing it was something else. She'd taken a lot of baby steps, and having dinner with him was a bigger step than before. There was no turning back.

The lounge was dark and empty though a row of patrons were lined up at the bar. Hunter found an empty booth in a dark corner and watched Lydia slide in. He sat across from her. A waitress arrived immediately and Hunter ordered the jambalaya.

"The chef is going to be delighted," the waitress said.

"We'll let him know how it is." Lydia took a sip of water and watched the waitress make her way back to the kitchen.

"Tell me about your childhood," Hunter said when they settled.

"It was terribly boring. I didn't think it was boring at the time, but every second of every hour was planned for me." Her eyes looked weary. "And my mother was always telling me who I could be friends with, who to avoid, what parties I needed to go to and what boys were off-limits."

"You're right, your childhood sounded boring."

"What about you?"

"My childhood was awesome. With the exception of the death of my parents, it was great." He searched back for his memories. "We lived in Henderson on a dirt road. At the end of the road there was this really sharp incline up to the connecting street. My brothers and sister and I used to climb up the incline with our bikes and then ride it down despite all the deep rain gullies and pock-marked areas." He closed his eyes, reliving the thrill of those wild rides.

"You were allowed to play outside?" Her eyes took on a round, open expression.

He grinned. "If I hadn't met your parents, I'd think you were joking."

"No." She shook her head. "Outside was dirty and hot and humid. My mother's favorite saying was that ladies learned to serve tea, arrange flowers and dress appropriately. Ladies do not perspire. I have a huge long list of what ladies don't do. But since we need to eventually go to bed, we'll just avoid that. There are more things on my mother's list of what ladies don't do than what they can do."

"I'm going to make it all up to you."

Her eyebrows rose. And her heart rate kicked up. What could that possibly mean? The very thought excited her. "What did you have in mind?"

"We're going to head to the hot springs later and dig in the dirt."

"Really!" She couldn't stop herself from smiling.

"I spent a lot of time making mud and building buildings. In Las Vegas sand, that wasn't always easy."

The waitress brought their jambalaya and delicately hovered without seeming to hover. And after the first forkful, Lydia smiled. "This is delicious. My compliments to Chef Mauro."

The waitress dimpled and left to pass on Lydia's message.

"Not bad," Hunter said.

Suddenly a huge commotion broke out from the door to the casino.

Hunter frowned. A few patrons went to the entrance to peer inside. Someone was shouting at the top of their lungs and a slot machine made a large number of loud dings.

Lydia peered over her shoulder. "I wonder what happened."

Filtering through to them were shouts of "I won! I won!"

"Let's go see." Hunter slid out of the booth and Lydia followed him.

"I won," came an excited man's voice.

Hunter shoved his way through the crowd surrounding a slot machine. It was one of the progressive machines linked to all the other progressive machines at all the other casinos. The pit boss arrived to turn off the bells and whistles.

"I won." David's hand shot up into the air. "Thirty-eight thousand dollars."

Leon joined his brother and the two stared at the slot machine. David took out his phone and snapped a photo of the slot machine.

"Congratulations," Lydia said.

Hunter shrugged. He supposed it was only a matter of time before one of them won something, considering how long and how much they played.

"Come right this way," Lydia said, indicating the pit boss, who opened a hole in the wall of spectators. "And not only can you collect your winnings, but we'll take care of your IRS obligation, too."

David's eyes narrowed. "You mean I have to pay the taxes before I can collect?"

"There's no free money in Reno," Hunter said, stepping in smoothly, "and you do want to keep this all legal, don't you?"

A mutinous looked showed in David's eyes. "Of course," he mumbled, "on the up and up." He exchanged looks with his brother and stamped off after the pit boss.

"That was almost petty, Lydia," Hunter said as they made their way back to the lounge to finish their dinner.

"Yes, it was. And it's on my mother's 'not to do' list."

She slid into the booth and picked up her fork. "But it kinda felt good."

Hunter burst out laughing. "And you should be so ashamed."

She grinned back, almost breathless at his overwhelming joy. "I will be...later."

Chapter 8

Lydia was exhausted. Maya had awakened her at the crack of dawn asking for a proper rodeo outfit. After a morning with her tutor, then a riding lesson, Lydia had taken her daughter shopping for that perfect outfit to wear to a rodeo. Lydia had to concede her daughter looked darling.

Maya pranced in front of her mom. "Do I look okay?" She wore purple jeans, purple cowboy boots, a bedazzled white shirt and a purple child-sized Stetson. Purple was Maya's new favorite color.

"You look perfect." Lydia adjusted the collar on her shirt. She'd popped for new black-and-white boots for herself and had to admit, they did look perfect with her designer jeans and plain white cotton shirt. Maya had tried to talk her into a pink Stetson, but Lydia declined. Boots were enough for her.

A knock sounded at the door and Maya ran to open it. Hunter stepped into the foyer. He wore jeans, hiking boots, a white shirt and a baseball cap.

Maya gave him a critical look and frowned. "You don't look much like a cowboy."

He grinned at her. "This is as cowboy as I'm going to get. And you're very…purple."

Maya preened. "I love purple."

"And purple seems to love you."

Maya giggled.

Lydia hid her smile, liking the way that Hunter treated her daughter as a real person.

They rode the elevator down to the lobby. Two security guards dressed in casual jeans and shirts fell into step behind them. Lydia hated that Maya couldn't go anywhere without security. For a moment, her anger at Leon and David rose all over again.

"That's you're cranky face," Hunter said.

"I'm still upset that we can't go anywhere without some sort of security. Maya should be able to just be a kid."

"It's only temporary." He reached out and touched her shoulder.

Heat swirled around her skin, not enough to dissipate her anger, but enough to make her more aware of his seductive presence. "I don't care. It's just so wrong."

A valet parked Hunter's car at the curb. A black SUV fell in behind them. Maya opened the back door and bounced inside. By the time Lydia had settled into the passenger seat, Maya was asking how far the fairgrounds were.

"Ten minutes, short stuff," Hunter said. "Lydia, did you buy the house?"

"I made the offer this morning. I'm hoping the owner will accept it. I'm paying cash for the house, so escrow should be quick." The Realtor, Margaret, had been surprised at Lydia's cash offer, but she needed things to move quickly to get Maya settled.

A long line of cars waited to get into the fairgrounds. Hunter found a parking spot. The walk to the stands was a bit long, but Maya twisted and turned to look at everything.

The fairgrounds were alive with carnival rides at one side of the arena, a food court in the center behind the general seating stands. Long rows of barns were situated behind the reserved seating areas.

"It sort of smells here," Lydia said when they found their seats at the center of the arena. The two security guards placed themselves directly behind them.

"That's what happens when you involve horses and cattle." Hunter sat down on the bench, holding the schedule in his hand.

Maya stood at the railing, hanging over the top rail, bouncing up and down in excitement.

Hunter looked over the schedule of events. "This evening's events are calf-roping, barrel racing and steer riding by the junior and senior rodeo entrants."

Lydia looked around. The stands were slowly filling up. Rodeo was big business in Reno. Lydia marveled at the number of people who packed the stands, anticipatory looks on their faces. This was her community now and she was going to have to be a part of it for Maya's sake. And there was a part of her that wondered if the hotel could capitalize on this.

A line of horse and rides began to form. Lydia leaned forward to watch. Obviously the rodeo was starting with a little parade.

"Mom, there's Patti." Maya waved frantically and after a moment, Patti waved back.

Patti sat at the front of the long line of horses, the Nevada flag attached to her saddle somehow. Lydia couldn't quite figure out how. A boy a little younger than Patti angled his big horse next to hers. He held an American flag attached to his saddle.

"Ladies and gentlemen," came a voice from a raised podium. "Please stand for the national anthem." A young woman stood at the microphone and somewhere music began to play. The woman opened her mouth and began to sing. As she sang, the young riders paraded around the arena.

When Patti and her horse came even with their seats, Maya yelled and waved. Patti grinned, but looked straight ahead.

At the end of the national anthem, everyone was allowed to sit down. The first event, breakaway calf roping, was announced—first the girls, then the boys by age.

Lydia didn't think she'd be interested in this, but she was. Caught by the excitement of the crowd, she found herself cheering the young ropers on, amazed at their skills. After the breakaway calf roping was goat tying. Lydia didn't quite understand the purpose of it, but she cheered just the same. Then riders raced around poles. Finally the barrel racing. When Patti was announced, Maya went wild. She cheered, jumped up and down and clapped.

"She's having a good time." Hunter commented.

"Amazingly enough, I am too." Lydia watched at Patti raced around the barrels. She finished her course and after a few seconds her time was displayed on a board.

"This is so much fun," Maya said. "I want to be in a rodeo, Mom."

"Me, too," Lydia replied.

"I don't think I'd mind being in one myself," Hunter added.

Maya and Lydia started laughing and Hunter just grinned.

The rodeo eventually came to an end. Lydia, Maya and Hunter made their way to the gate only to be stopped by Patti.

"Hey," Patti said, "I thought you'd like to meet my dad."

"I'd like to meet him," Maya said with a glance at her mother, a query in her eyes.

"Of course, I want to meet him, too," Lydia said.

"Come on." Patti grabbed Maya's hand.

Hunter, Lydia and Maya followed Patti behind the stands to the barns. A short, muscular man stood leaning against the open door of a stall patting the horse's head that poked out.

"Dad," Patti called. "These are our new neighbors."

"Hi, I'm Hector Ibarra, Patti's dad."

"I'm Lydia Montgomery. This is my daughter, Maya, and my friend Hunter Russell." Lydia held out her hand. "I have a lot of questions to ask."

"I want to be in the rodeo," Maya said. "I want to do what Patti does. Can you teach me?"

Hector Ibarra grinned at Maya. "I can teach you." He raised his eyebrows, his eyes questioning. "Ms. Montgomery…"

"Lydia…" she said.

"Lydia, I've been teaching barrel racing, calf roping and pole bending for over twenty years. Anything that goes at a rodeo, I can teach."

"I need a horse," Maya said.

Hector laughed. "I can help you with that, too."

Maya looked so happy Lydia wanted to cry. Shame on David and Leon for trying to force Maya to be what she didn't want to be. Maya could be a lady and rodeo queen if she wanted. Hell, Lydia wanted to be the rodeo queen too. Not a bad thing.

The drive home was quiet. Maya had fallen asleep.

"I like it here," Lydia said to Hunter.

"Me, too."

"Are you thinking about staying?"

"I'm thinking about thinking about it," he replied with a sideways glance at her.

"Reno is growing. I'm sure this town could use a good

architect." She couldn't hide the hope in her voice. Hunter had become a fixture in her life.

Mitchell would have never let her and Maya go to a rodeo. Hunter had happily fallen in with their plans and sort of dressed the part. In fact, Hunter let her be herself. He didn't tell what to wear, what charities to be involved in, which business wives to court. He was perfectly comfortable with letting her explore what she wanted.

She studied him. His face was illuminated in the lights from the dashboard. He was man who was comfortable with himself. Any woman would be lucky to have him. Why not someone like her? Lydia turned that thought over in her mind.

She'd come to Reno to stand on her own two feet, to learn to be independent. She wasn't completely functional yet, but would be. Hunter encouraged her. He didn't tell her no over anything. Mitchell always had a long list of things she couldn't be involved in just like her parents. If any activity didn't further his career or social standing, she wasn't allowed to do it. Mitchell used to have a running commentary about everyone and everything. Who was wealthier than him? Whose kids were in trouble? Whose businesses were in trouble? Which spouse was unfaithful? He knew more about the seamy underside of New Orleans society than anyone Lydia had ever known.

Mitchell would never have allowed Lydia to strike up a friendship with Hector Ibarra and his daughter. He would have been scandalized because Hector did not come with the proper social pedigree, unless he saw a reason to be friends with the Ibarra family. Hector seemed like a nice person and Patti definitely was. Lydia was determined to know them better. Her life had been limited and she needed to expand her horizons. She wanted her daughter to be open to the possibility of things. Lydia refused to limit her daughter's friendships or her future.

The next day Lydia mother found her in her office. "We need some mother/daughter time." Caroline looked elegant is a peach floral sundress that contrasted with her cocoa colored skin.

"Okay," Lydia responded, uncertain what her mother had in mind. Lydia had plans to check out a spa at another hotel. She wanted to check out the competition. "I plan to check out a spa today."

"Oh, good, I'll come along." Caroline clapped her hands.

Lydia viewed her mother with suspicion. "That would be lovely."

"And we can do lunch afterward."

"Sounds fine," Lydia replied. She called the hotel and booked a massage for two along with a mani-pedi. As she drove to the hotel, her mother chattered, keeping everything light and friendly while saying absolutely nothing. Lydia found herself waiting, wondering if her mother's artless conversation would lead to something.

The Tambien hotel was small in contrast to the larger hotels. But the spa was elegance incarnate. Spanish tile floors with white wicker furniture and green palm plants in huge pink urns greeted them as they walked in. The receptionist signed them in and escorted them to their massage.

The massage suite was large, painted a soothing beige, yet dimly lit. Soft, soothing music sounded. Candles decorated a long counter, their scent heavy in the air. The room contained two massage tables.

And all the while Caroline continued to talk.

"You remember Collier Grant," Caroline said as they lay on the massage tables. "Everyone just found out that he's being sued by his former mistress for breach of contract. I just can't understand Collier getting involved with a cocktail waitress. She is working her way through law school, but he promised to pay for her school and then signed a cocktail napkin stating his intention."

Collier was never the brightest bulb on the Christmas tree. She wondered how his parents were dealing with his stupidity.

"And then," Caroline said, interrupting Lydia's flow of thought. "Kate West is getting divorced, again, for the fourth time."

"She's what...only forty years old."

"My dear, she's thirty-five. Can you imagine four husbands in eleven years? I really thought the one with the tennis pro would last...more than a year."

Lydia tried not to snicker. Kate West had never been much for longevity.

"Kate just doesn't have the fortitude to make it through the hard time."

Lydia shook her head as the massage therapist worked on her arms. "Kate is a romantic. She thinks marriage is a constant honeymoon and as soon as the reality sets in, she's done." Lydia had liked Kate. Kate lived her life according to her rules and Lydia had been constantly controlled by other people's rules.

"And let me tell you about Millicent Avery. She's had so many plastic surgeries she can't blink her eyes anymore."

Lydia closed her eyes and let her thoughts drift. Her mother continued to dish out gossip as though Lydia were truly interested. In fact Lydia was bored. She didn't care one bit about who was doing what in New Orleans. What did care about was what her mother was leading up to. If Caroline thought that telling her all this gossip was going to make Lydia homesick, she needed to rethink her strategy.

Lydia didn't miss New Orleans one bit, nor did she miss the gossip. The gossip was nothing new. Her mother always seemed to know what was going on, and this was the total aspect of her conversation, as though all this stuff was important. This was what Lydia's life had been before and she was rather ashamed of herself for participating in the gossip, the backstabbing and the delight when other people fell from prominence.

She thought about Maya and the relationship she had with her daughter. She and Maya talked about things that mattered, that made Maya a better person. She didn't want her daughter to be caught up in people's personal trivia. The world didn't turn on gossip, despite her mother's assurance that gossip had its place. Lydia's world had changed. She liked the direction it was going.

After the rodeo last night, Maya had talked about nothing but horses. In the space of a few hours, she'd learned everything she could about the care and feeding of horses, the breeds she was interested in and the rodeo. Lydia was as enthusiastic as her daughter. She wanted her daughter to participate in activities that would make her a better person.

"And I'm sure you heard about Elliot Johns. He and his wife divorced. When you come home, I'll set up a lunch for you and Elliot. Since he's on the market again and you're on the market…" Her mother gave her a sly wink.

No. Lydia disliked Elliot Johns as much as she disliked Leon and David. Never again would she marry for social position. She wanted to tell her mother her feelings, but it would just start an argument, with Caroline telling Lydia she didn't know what she needed for herself.

As her mother rambled on, her thoughts drifted to

Hunter. He was so different from the people she had associated with in New Orleans. He was real. He didn't tell her she was being silly, or that she didn't know her own mind. He liked Maya, and Maya liked him. Whenever she saw him, Maya immediately gravitated toward him. And when she talked, he listened. Lydia knew that one day he would make a good father.

Once the massage was over, Lydia and her mother went to another room set up for mani-pedis. Caroline chose coral nail lacquer for her finger and toe nails to match her sundress. Lydia chose clear.

Caroline liked the Tambien hotel and suggested the main restaurant. Lydia agreed even though she wanted to get away. Her mother's constant chatter grated on her. The desire for her mother to strengthen their bond left Lydia feeling claustrophobic. She'd left New Orleans for Reno to be independent and now her parents wanted to pull her back.

The Tambien's restaurant had a modern, upscale look to it with lots of silver paint, chrome edges and dark wood tables. The booths were upholstered in maroon with silver accents and the floor was a black-and-gray-veined marble tile. The waitstaff wore black pants and shirts with white ties. The menus looked like books with lists of the dishes separated by silver scrolled lines. All Lydia wanted was a hamburger and fries.

Caroline excused herself to use the restroom. She watched her mother's graceful movements across the room. Lydia needed a break from her mother's gossip and constant hints about moving back to New Orleans. Lydia wasn't moving back. She liked her new life and she felt a confrontation building that she would do anything to avoid. Her parents were going to be hurt by her decision.

Lydia used the reprieve to text Hunter and ask him to text her back in fifteen minutes with some sort of emergency. Any manufactured emergency would do so she could claim an end to this mother/daughter moment to avoid the unpleasantness she felt coming. Her mother returned, her makeup flawlessly reapplied, and slid smoothly into her chair. "You should at least put on some lipstick, Lydia. Your face needs some color."

"I'm fine, Mom," Lydia replied while she glanced through the menu. She'd stopped wearing makeup and her skin felt clean and fresh.

The waitress hovered while her mother dithered over the menu. "I can't decide if I want the garden salad or the tomato and cucumber appetizer."

"Mom." Lydia's frustration bubbled to the surface. "Just pick something. I'm ready." She glanced at the waitress, who smiled politely.

Caroline looked startled. "I'll have a plain garden salad, no dressing," she said. "I'll just drink my water."

"And I'll the bacon avocado burger, sweet potato fries and large lemonade."

The waitress nodded, taking their order.

"Are you sure you want a hamburger, Lydia? It's so messy. If you get grease on that lovely blouse, it'll be ruined. When you return to New Orleans to help campaign for your dad's mayoral run for New Orleans, you won't be able to indulge in hamburgers. They are so fattening."

Lydia's hand paused in the act of squeezing lemon into her water, not certain she'd heard correctly. "Dad is running for mayor of New Orleans!" So this is what David and Leon had been alluding to. She should have tried to find out more, but she'd been busy and somehow the thought had been pushed into a far corner of her mind.

"Of course, didn't he tell you?" Caroline's half smile

curved her lips, but little enthusiasm showed in her eyes. "He's so thrilled to be asked. He's always wanted a career in politics and now the time is just right. You must ask him about his campaign. He has such progressive ideas for how New Orleans should be run."

Though her mother's voice was light, Lydia detected strain behind the words. Lydia leaned over the edge of the table. "Let me get this clear. Dad is running for mayor?"

"I just told you."

So that was the real reason behind the mother/daughter spa time.

"We must present a united front, which is why you must come home, dear." Caroline cut off a tiny slice of bread from the basket between them. She daintily nibbled at the edges. "This is very good bread." She put the piece down on the bread plate and then ignored it.

"Why is Dad running for mayor?" Lydia sliced a huge chunk of bread and lathered it with butter, to her mother's disapproval. She paused a second and added more butter. She knew she was being childish, but couldn't seem to stop herself. Wise, Caroline said nothing.

"I just said, because he wants to." Caroline leaned closer to Lydia. "And it would be so amazing to live in the mayor's mansion. Think of the parties we could have, the people who would attend. Who knows what might happen. Mayor today, then governor and possibly a senator with a mansion in Georgetown." She busied herself placing her napkin on her lap. "You know, you would make the perfect senator's wife. Think of it, Lydia, travel all over the world, dinner with celebrities, being a guest at the White House." Caroline sighed.

Again a slight, patronizing smile from her mother made Lydia cringe.

Lydia blinked. She didn't want to live in Washington,

D.C. She didn't want a senator for a husband. She didn't want to return to New Orleans. She didn't want to present "a united front," as her mother said. She didn't want her parents interfering in her life.

"Is that all I am to you?" Lydia asked, trying to keep the surge of anger filling her under control.

Her mother's eyebrows rose. "What do you mean, dear?"

"I'm really nothing but a commodity to be used to further whatever Dad wants." Lydia studied her mother. "But then again, that's all you are. A commodity. A…" Lydia's phone rang before she could say anything she would regret later. She glanced at it. Hunter was calling. *Thank you, Hunter.* "Excuse me, I have to take this."

"Let it go to voice mail, Lydia. You and I are discussing something very important. Your future."

More important than all the gossip from New Orleans. "You and I can finish this discussion later." She answered the phone.

"Are you all right?" Hunter asked.

No, she wasn't all right, but couldn't say that in front of her mother. "I don't know how to answer that question right now."

"Do you need me to rescue you?"

"Yes," Lydia replied, knowing she sounded desperate. Suddenly, she needed to get away from her mother and the gentle insinuations that she was not only ruining her life, but Maya's life and her parents' lives. And possibly the future of New Orleans. Maybe even the United States. How had her decision to take charge of her future suddenly become equivalent to the *fall of the Roman Empire*?

"Are you still at the Tambien?"

"Yes."

"Hang on, Lydia. I'll be there in ten minutes."

Lydia disconnected. "Mom, you stay and finish your lunch." She flagged the waitress and handed her fifty dollars.

"But…" Her mother flailed about for words.

"This is for lunch," Lydia told the waitress. "Keep the change." She gathered up her purse and dug inside.

"Is something wrong with Maya?" Caroline asked a panicked look on her face.

"Maya is fine," Lydia said. "It's something else. Here are the keys to my car. Hunter is picking me up." Lydia slid out of the booth. "Sorry, Mom." She kissed her mother on the cheek, clutched her purse to her and rushed out of the restaurant before her mother could object.

By the time Hunter arrived, Lydia was so angry she shook. She took two tries before she could open the door and slide into the passenger seat.

"Lydia?" Hunter asked, concern in his tone.

"Just drive. I don't care where, just drive."

"Do you want ice cream, or a bar?" He eased his Mercedes into traffic while Lydia pondered his question.

"Ice cream is safer," she said.

"I know just the place." He made his way through Reno to the freeway and turned south, zipping away from Reno.

Lydia leaned back against the car seat and closed her eyes, replaying the scene with her mother over and over again. She wanted to scream, to pound her hands on something. She wanted to grab Maya and run as far away as she could get and never be found again. Her life belonged to her, not her parents. Maya's life belonged to her and not Lydia or her parents.

She closed her eyes and let the miles roll by, thankful Hunter asked no questions. At some point she dozed. When she opened her eyes again, they were in South Lake Tahoe, cruising down a road bordering the crystal clear water.

She didn't know much about Lake Tahoe, but she did know it was supposed to be one of the clearest lakes in the world with some of the most beautiful beaches. And from the rows of huge homes right on the beach, other people agreed with her.

The ice cream shop in South Lake Tahoe sported a cutesy sign that contained pink decorations surrounding the name Hot Ice. The shop sat on a small pier jutting out over the water. Hunter parked the car in an adjacent lot and they followed a winding path, bordered by blooming marigolds, leading up to the building.

Inside the shop was a profusion of color with pink being dominant. A long row of refrigerated cases showed huge containers of homemade ice cream of over fifty flavors along with rows of cans containing different toppings.

Lydia ordered her favorite, chocolate cheesecake with chocolate chips and whipped cream. Hunter ordered triple chocolate brownie with double fudge sauce and whipped cream. Lydia stared at his choice. She tilted her head to watch him as the attendant scooped the chocolate ice cream into a double sized bowl.

He caught her watching him and grinned. "I love chocolate."

"I can see." She found herself grinning back, her anger easing.

"Let's sit outside," he said, opening a side door leading to a wood patio.

Lydia sat at a wrought-iron table with an umbrella. Hunter tilted the umbrella slightly to block the early afternoon sun and sat across from her. The air was warm, but a breeze off the lake cooled them.

"You seem a lot upset." Hunter dug his spoon into his ice cream. "What happened?"

"My father has decided to run for mayor of New Orleans and my choices are to return and avoid a scandal, or turn my daughter over to Sleazy and Sleazier to avoid a scandal so that his campaign is not tainted by a daughter who refuses to get with the program." She licked the ice cream on her spoon. She was in chocolate heaven.

"You have a third choice."

"And that would be?" One eyebrow lifted at the idea she had any choices at all.

"Get massive amounts of plastic surgery and run off to Papua New Guinea to hide in the rain forests with isolated tribes. No clothes allowed."

Lydia sighed. "Excluding my disdain for the great outdoors, that is looking like a viable option." She stared at the lake, the breeze ruffling the edges of her hair. She felt as though her mother had betrayed her.

"I can come with some great ideas," Hunter said with a chuckle.

A boat glided by with a man at the helm and a woman in a super skimpy bikini laying on a deck chair getting the sun. A second boat raced parallel to the shore, towing a skier, her long hair flying behind her as she skimmed the water. Further out, jet skiers bounced against the waves.

"Why is it that every parent I've ever met wants their children to grow up and be independent, except for mine?" She dug her spoon into her ice cream and pulled out a chunk.

"Miss E. raised my siblings and I to be very independent, so I don't think I can even find an answer that would help you."

Mountains ringed the lake, rising high into the clear sky. Lydia traced the line of their peaks against the blue-

ness and wished she lived on one as far from her parents
as she could get.

"It's almost as if being independent implies I don't love
them anymore." At the moment she was finding it hard to
love them at all.

"Being an only child can be tough," he said.

A young man and woman walked the beach arm in arm.
Honeymooners, Lydia thought. A family of five frolicked
in the waves. The mother, a matronly looking woman with
a ready smile, joined in her children's play. Caroline would
never be caught playing in a lake. Her idea of recreational
swimming was the luxurious pool at her country club with
lots of wine and sunscreen. *We may be people of color,
but we still get sunburned,* her mother often admonished.

Lydia's exasperation boiled to the surface. "My mother
wants me to be her clone, and my father wants me to be
totally dependent, obedient and subservient. That attitude
is so archaic." And yet when Lydia looked at some of the
women in her social set, that's exactly what they were,
clones of each other—pampered and self-indulgent.

Hunter opened and closed his mouth a couple of times,
before jamming more ice cream in his mouth. "I'm a guy,"
he finally said after two full spoonfuls disappeared into
his mouth, "and this is uncharted territory for me, but my
opinion is, you have to be who you are."

"Who am I?" Lydia had thought she'd known who she
was when she married Mitchell, but in reality she had been
nothing but an extension of her husband. Everything he
did, said or thought came first. Anything she did, said or
thought meant nothing unless it enhanced his career or
standing in the community. And she had allowed that because at the time that was who she thought she was. That
was who her mother said she was.

"You're a beautiful, smart, amazing woman who has a

part ownership in a casino. You're mother to an awesome daughter and…" he paused licking his spoon "…you're a person I want to be with."

Her eyes went wide. "Why? Why would you want to be with me?"

"All of the above reasons, plus I like your moxie."

"I didn't come with a backbone. You would not have said any of those things about me a year ago."

"Doesn't matter who you were, just who you are now." Hunter took her hand and squeezed it.

She finished her ice cream, feeling calmer. For all his words, she still wasn't sure who she was, but she was going to find out.

Chapter 9

Hunter knocked on his grandmother's office door and opened it when she called for him to enter. She'd texted him a message to come immediately and he'd dropped everything.

Miss E. had taken over Jasper's old office, a large and comfortable room with a walnut desk at one end, matching bookcases behind it and a sitting area that currently contained his grandmother on a yellow sofa with Jasper next to her and Scott sitting on one of two matching chairs flanking the sofa. A picture window showed the city of Reno. The view was spectacular.

Hunter took the second chair and settled in, crossing his legs, watching his grandmother.

Jasper held a paper in his hands. "I don't understand. She's saying I'm insane. My own daughter, my own flesh and blood." His gray-white hair stood on end as though he'd raked his hands through it repeatedly. His blue eyes were weary, and his mouth drooped.

Miss E. patted his arm. "Calm down, Jasper. First things first, you're going to talk to Vanessa. I already have a call in to her office, but she's in court and won't be back for another couple of hours."

"What's going on?" Hunter asked curiously. He'd been

expecting a report on David and Leon, not this new development.

Jasper handed him the paper he held. Hunter scanned it. "A competency hearing!"

Jasper scrubbed his face with his hands. "My daughter is furious that I put the casino and hotel up for grabs in a poker game. She feels I should have given it to her."

"Okay, I'm going to play devil's advocate here." Hunter handed the paper back to Jasper. "It was sort of odd that you put the ownership of this place into a poker game."

Jasper balled the paper up and looked like he would toss it into the trash. Miss E. took it away from him and smoothed it out again.

"I owned ninety-five percent of this casino. My daughter owned five percent, which I gave her. Next to burning it down or blowing it up, I could do whatever I wanted with it."

"True," Scott said. "But it was a peculiar enough action. Do you think she might have a point?"

"No," Jasper snarled. "My daughter is a spoiled little brat who wanted to keep the money rolling in because she felt entitled to it. Until I got rid of the casino, she was absolutely, positively happy just getting a check. She didn't want to run it. When I said I was getting rid of it, she was originally on board, expecting a big payout, until she realized I planned to gamble it away in the poker game."

"How do we handle this, Scott?" Hunter asked his brother.

"I'll start digging into your daughter's background. I have a feeling something else is going on and we don't know what that is." Scott took the notice from Miss E. and scanned it, frowning slightly.

"Like what?" Jasper asked.

"What do you know about your daughter's personal life?" Scott asked.

"I try not to butt into her life."

"She doesn't appear to have the same respect for yours." Miss E. laid a hand gently on Jasper's shoulder. He looked at her, his blue eyes watery, a worried frown wrinkling his face.

"How worried do I need to be about this competency hearing?" Jasper asked.

"You're a big personality and people seem to expect you to be a little odd," Miss E. said, "and until you do something that irritates them, they are happy to let you be who you need to be. Why didn't you just give the casino to your daughter?"

"She would have broken it up and sold it for parts." Jasper took Miss E.'s hands in his. "You respect and love the business and I was delighted when you won. I knew you would keep the tradition going."

"And the business has been good to me," Miss E. said.

"Who knew," Hunter said, "that your one little decision, would generate so much controversy. Lydia's stepsons are here about money and her parents are here about money. And know your daughter is throwing her hat into the ring because of the money."

"It's a good thing we were never rich," Scott said. "All this money is causing nothing but animosity and greed."

"No," Miss E. said, shaking her head. "The money was just a catalyst. All those feelings were already there."

Jasper's shoulders slumped. "I was so busy building this casino, I left my daughter in my ex-wife's hands. Not my smartest move. I showed my affection with money. She probably thinks because I didn't give her the casino, I don't love her."

Hunter glanced at Scott. Scott rolled his eyes and Hunter suppressed a smile. Scott just didn't get all this emotional stuff. Or maybe it made him uncomfortable.

"She's acting out," Hunter said. He understood why. After his parents' death, he'd done the same thing. He'd felt abandoned. "She probably thinks you've abandoned her. The only link you had with your daughter was the casino and now she doesn't have that at all."

Jasper looked surprised at Hunter's statement. "But I love her. I'm sure she knows that."

"Have you told her?" Miss pressed her hand into Jasper's.

Jasper sighed. "Maybe not in so many words." He stood and straightened his tie, looking determined. "I need to find my daughter. I have to fix this." He walked to the door, stopped, his head bowed. Then he gripped the doorknob, twisted it open and left.

After he left, Scott rose to get himself a glass of water. When he sat again, he reached for his iPad on the table and activated it. "So do you want to hear what I found out about David and Leon?

Miss E. sighed. "Honestly, there's a part of me that doesn't want to hear."

"I could just highlights. Which do you want first, the misdemeanors or the felonies?"

"I need a glass of whiskey."

"Do we need to find a bar?"

Miss E. stood, went to her desk and opened a side drawer to pull out a bottle of whiskey. She set it on the table with a tiny thump. "My 'break in case of an emergency' bottle."

"Then break it open, Grams," Scott said. "This is an emergency."

Miss E. poured three glasses and handed one to Scott and another to Hunter. She sat down, closed her eyes and took a sip.

"Money makes a person crazy," Scott said as he swiped

the screen of his iPad. "David and Leon are a boatload of crazy." He swiped the screen again. "Okay, first of all, I have an army buddy who owns a security agency in Baton Rouge." His gaze shifted to Miss E. "You are going to owe a boatload of bucks to pay this guy."

"What did he find out?" Miss E. asked.

"These two started breaking the law while still in the cradle. Breaking and entering, car theft and bullying. Daddy covered this all up. Nothing made the papers, no records, no arrests and no convictions. Daddy greased a lot of palms to keep these two out of trouble." Scott referred back to the screen. "There were allegations of spousal abuse, adultery, drug use. Basically, your model citizen type behavior."

"They sound charming," Hunter said with a frown.

"Leon has been cited for three driving under the influence infractions. David has two citations."

"I don't understand," Miss E. said. "How do they expect the court to give them custody of Maya?"

"Because…" Scott tapped the arm of his chair. "They know how to work the system. They've been doing that since they were seven years old. Lydia's a nice woman, but she's a guppy about to go swimming with sharks."

"We have to tip the scale in her favor," Miss E. said firmly.

"I send a copy of this report to Vanessa Peabody. She'll know how to use it."

"This is all circumstantial," Hunter said. "People have been paid off to look the other way."

"Maybe, but I think I have an ace in the hole."

Hunter's eyebrows rose. "What?"

"I'm working on a few things." Scott refused to divulge more. "And we should have the DNA results shortly. There was a small mix-up at the lab, which caused a small delay, but they're on it now."

Miss E. took a long sip of her whiskey. "This is sad. Here we are strangers protecting Lydia. Her parents should be taking care of her. Not only is this a shame that they aren't, but immoral."

Hunter shook his head. He filled them in about her father's political aspirations.

"The more interesting question is," Scott put in, "why are her parents working with David and Leon? I have to ponder that for a while." He pushed himself to his feet.

Hunter rose, too, wondering the same thing. "They're conspiring against Lydia. I don't know how, I don't know why. But we're going to find out."

"Then do it," Miss E. said firmly. "Lydia and Maya have become precious to me, and her family will have to go through me to get to them, and nobody hurts what's mine."

Chapter 10

Lydia tilted her head one way and then the next, studying the three-dimensional model of the spa Hunter had built.

"The entrance is here," he said, pointing to a door in the center, "which opens into the reception area. Whole body massage rooms are to the right. The full service salon is to the left. Once that salon is working, we'll close the salon in the hotel."

"I don't think we should do that. Some women just want a quick hairstyle. I suggest we change the salon over to just hairstyling and manicures, and make the spa a full service area."

Hunter nodded. "Good idea. I'll make a note of that. Behind the reception area is a corridor that leads directly to the sauna and hot tubs which will pump water from the hot springs."

"Lovely." Lydia knew spas. She and her mother had had a standing appointment for the salon in the country club weekly. "I know someone who would be perfect to run this place."

"Who would that be?"

"Nicole Edwards. The salon I went to is a family business and since Nicole isn't family, there is no opportunity for her to advance. She's exceptional and would be perfect. I think we should contact her immediately because she'll know all the details that need to be in place that I don't know."

"Let's run it by Miss E. and see what she says. We could hire her on as a consultant until the spa is built."

"I like that." Lydia walked around the table looking at the model from all angles. "I'll talk to Miss E. as soon as we're done."

He showed her the blueprints, explaining what everything meant. He included his idea of what the inside should look like through a series of drawings. Lydia was amazed. Hunter was a very talented artist. "This isn't bad. I'm a little surprised that it has such a feminine look to it."

"Dudes are not going to go to a spa."

"Where do they go? Man cave spas?" Lydia said.

Hunter laughed. "That's not a bad idea. But most hotels I stay in have male personnel that will go to a man's room."

Lydia liked watching Hunter laugh. His eyes crinkled up and his mouth had this quirky look to it. Mitchell seldom laughed, as though laughing wasn't manly. And when he'd smiled, it had usually been over something Maya had done he thought cute.

"How are you holding up?" Hunter said, changing the subject.

Lydia paused to think about his question. Resilience had never been her strong suit. Hunter had told her she was hanging tough. "I had no idea I was so strong. Maya shows no sign of stress. Miss E. is so good at keeping her occupied, I don't think she worries."

"Which for Scott and I has been a blessing and a curse."

"I don't understand."

"She wants great-grandchildren. And she wants them tomorrow."

"So Maya is a place-holder," Lydia said.

Hunter burst out laughing again. "No kidding."

"She adores Miss E.," Lydia continued. "My mother spends all her time correcting Maya, giving her deportment lessons and explaining why a lady needs to be act a certain way. Miss E. spends time encouraging her to try to new things, have an adventure and get dirty. I love my mother, but I'd trade her in for Miss E. without one thought."

"Miss E. may sound like she's a pied piper, but she can lower the hammer without a moment's notice." Hunter's face took a faraway look as though remembering some childhood transgression that brought the "hammer." "It wasn't all sunshine and pony rides for us."

"Miss E. wasn't worried about reputations, social status or charity work. You got to be children. Me, I was a minadult. If I didn't know better, I could have sworn my mother had herself cloned."

"Your mother was doing what she thought was best for her and for you. She grew up in a world where stuff like that mattered. Miss E. may have been a great poker player and we never lacked for anything, but I used to worry about her because she had no other skills. If for any reason she was banned from playing poker, our world would have disintegrated."

"In her defense," Lydia said, "she made sure you all had skills so that you wouldn't be stuck like her. Knowing she had no fallback position must have been frightening for her."

"She never let it show," Hunter conceded.

Lydia's phone rang. She glanced at the display. "It's Vanessa."

"Go ahead and answer."

"Hello," Lydia said.

"I have the DNA results." Vanessa sounded worried.

"Okay, what is the result?" Lydia had managed to contain her curiosity, but now it returned.

"You need to come into the office. Leon and David's lawyer is meeting me at two. I need you to be at this meeting."

Lydia glanced at her watch. "Will David and Leon be there?"

"No, they declined my invitation. They just want their lawyer to handle everything."

"Can I bring Hunter?"

"That's fine," Vanessa said.

"I'll be there." Lydia disconnected and turned to Hunter. "She has the DNA results, but won't tell me anything. Will you come with me to meet with her and the other lawyer? The meeting's at two."

"Not a problem." Hunter started rolling up the blueprints of the spa, storing them in a tube. He glanced at his watch. "I'll be at the front entrance in forty minutes. Is that enough time?"

Lydia's stomach clenched. Whatever was in those results, it wasn't good. "I'll be there."

She called Miss E. as she went up the elevator to her room, asking her if she would watch Maya for the afternoon, then she quickly changed into a pantsuit, ran a comb through her hair, splashed on makeup and was at the front door seconds before Hunter pulled up in his Mercedes.

Hunter kept glancing at Lydia as he wove through traffic on their way to the lawyer's office. She sat next to him, tense and still, her hands clenched into fists. Her face was a mask hiding whatever else she was feeling.

"I don't understand why Vanessa couldn't tell me this on the phone," Lydia said. "What could she possibly tell me that I don't know? Maya is Mitchell's child. No matter what David and Leon assert, I did not have an affair."

"Whatever the results are, Vanessa has your back."

"I resent the fact that someone has to have my back."

"We'll find out soon enough. You need to relax." Hunter braked at a red light. "You're going to blow a blood vessel before we get there."

Lydia leaned back, her head resting against the headrest, and closed her eyes. Lines of strain showed on her face. Hunter wanted to pull over and take her in his arms. He wanted to reassure her everything would work out.

He pulled into the parking structure adjacent to Vanessa Peabody's office.

Vanessa Peabody's office was a large, well-structured place. Hunter admired the design as he and Lydia checked in with the receptionist and were directed to the conference room.

The conference room was small and intimate with a table large enough for eight people. The walls were painted a soothing beige and modern art in a parade of colors hung from the walls.

Lydia sat down and Hunter sat next to her. He took her hand and she smiled nervously at him, her lips trembling no matter how hard she tried to look strong and brave.

The door opened and Vanessa walked in, a large file in her arms. A man walked in behind her and sat down across the table. Vanessa sat across from Lydia.

Hunter studied the man he figured to be Leon and David's lawyer. He was a slender man dressed in a designer suit complete with power tie and fashionably arranged medium brown hair. His gray eyes darted around the room, taking in Lydia with a look that made Hunter want to get up and punch him.

"This is Kramer O'Reilly." Vanessa waved a hand

vaguely in the man's direction. "Leon and David's lawyer. Mr. O'Reilly, this is Mrs. Lydia Montgomery and Mr. Hunter Russell, a friend of hers."

If Hunter had to find one word to describe O'Reilly, slick came to mind. Everything about him was a little too smooth, a little too used car salesman smarmy. He wouldn't want to meet this guy in a court of law.

"Ms. Montgomery," O'Reilly said. He glanced at Hunter, curiosity in his eyes as though trying to figure out just what place Hunter played in Lydia's drama.

Vanessa opened the file and pulled out a piece of paper, which she handed to Lydia. "This is the DNA results."

Lydia quickly read it, her frown deepening. "I don't understand this."

Vanessa gave a slight smile. "As it turns out, David and Leon have a different DNA sequence from Maya."

"And this means—?" Lydia asked.

"We're not certain." Vanessa glanced down at the file. "David's and Leon's results show they are brothers, but they aren't Maya's brothers."

"That's because," O'Reilly said with a smug look on his face, "Ms. Montgomery had an affair that resulted in Maya not being Mr. Montgomery's child."

Lydia went pale. She half rose. "That's not true."

Hunter put a hand on hers. She glanced at him and he nodded his head. Slowly, she sat back down and tried to look composed. He could see tears in the corners of her eyes.

"I don't think we know what to think yet," Vanessa said calmly. "We need to exhume Mitchell's body."

"No," O'Reilly said firmly. "David and Leon will not allow this."

"That's not their decision to make," Vanessa replied. "*Mrs*. Montgomery is sole executer of Mr. Montgomery's

estate, and she's the only one who can make that decision."
Vanessa searched through the papers until she found one
and pulled it out.

Lydia tensed. Hunter held her hand tightly. Her hand
had gone cold and stiff beneath his.

"I object," O'Reilly said.

"Over what?" Vanessa asked. "It's to Leon and David's
advantage to have this all settled."

O'Reilly glared at Vanessa. "It's already settled. The
DNA results show that Maya is not Mitchell's daughter."

"One could say that," Vanessa said, her smug expression
deepening, "or one could say the result show that David
and Leon aren't his sons."

"That's impossible. I have a deposition from their
mother stating unequivocally that they are Mitchell's sons."

"And you just heard Mrs. Montgomery say the same
thing." Vanessa put her hands down flat on the table. "Mr.
O'Reilly, I'm sure you've heard this old saying. 'There's
your side. There's my side. And there's the truth.' There
is only one way to settle this argument for good. My client, I'm sure, is willing to sign the paperwork ordering the
exhumation of her late husband to put this matter to rest."

"Draw up the papers," Lydia said.

Vanessa handed her several sheets of paper. "Already
done. Please look them over, but don't sign them where
you see the highlighted areas."

O'Reilly's face went red with anger. He leaned back
in his chair and took a number of deep breaths. "I want a
copy of the exhumation order."

Vanessa rifled through her pile again and handed him
a copy. "You'll also find a two letters, informing you of
the copy you've just received." She pulled out her phone
and dialed it. "Let me call my notary and we'll get this
show on the road."

"A notary," O'Reilly blustered. "Hardly necessary."

"Yes, it is," Vanessa said sweetly. "I want to make certain your clients understand every step we're taking so they can't cry foul later on."

O'Reilly's eyes narrowed. Vanessa continued smiling pleasantly.

"My clients," O'Reilly said, "have been entirely reasonable through this entire process."

Hunter resisted a snort. Reasonable was not a word he would apply to David and Leon.

"Your clients initiated this situation. I'm sure they would want to follow it through to the bitter end no matter what the results are."

O'Reilly glared at Vanessa. She radiated calm serenity. Lydia looked simply tired. Hunter wanted to put his arms around her and keep her safe.

After the notary left, O'Reilly gathered up his piles of paperwork and stamped out. Lydia watched him go with resignation.

"I'm sorry, Lydia," Vanessa said. "I know this is going to be more difficult than it started out to be."

Lydia shook her head. "I will do what needs to be done to keep my daughter out of their hands."

Hunter and Lydia took their leave of Vanessa. Back in the car, Hunter saw that Lydia's hands shook as she buckled her seat belt.

"It'll be all right." Hunter started the car and put it in gear.

"I heard the rumor about her."

"About who?"

"Gwendolyn, Leon and David's mother. Everyone talked about her stepping out on Mitchell, but I didn't believe any of them because the same rumors circulated about me." Lydia rested her head against the headrest and closed her eyes. "What if those rumors were true?"

"Sounds like they are," Hunter said. He stopped the car at the bottom of the parking garage ramp, waiting for traffic to clear.

"Maya does have some affection for them and to find out they aren't her brothers is going to be devastating."

"Children are resilient and she has you. She'll come through this okay." Hunter didn't think Maya would be as devastated at Lydia thought. But that wasn't what Lydia needed to hear. He needed to be a sympathetic friend. "I think you need to get away from all this. How about a dinner and show tonight?"

She studied him. "Are you asking me for a date?"

"Yes, I am."

She laughed and he was thrilled to hear it. "What did you have in mind?"

"*Hair* is at the Center for the Performing Arts."

She stared at him, eyes wide with surprise. *"Hair."*

"I am from San Francisco. The hippie culture is alive and well there."

"There's a blues concert at the park."

"Are you saying you'd rather go to a blues concert than see *Hair?*"

She smiled at him. "Yes."

"I'm game for that. How about we start with dinner at Harrah's and then head to the park for the concert?"

"Works for me."

She gave him a huge smile and his heart went into overdrive. She was so beautiful when she smiled.

Lydia had a date. A real date. Doing something she wanted to do instead of the proper society things her parents expected of her and later Mitchell. Mitchell had once asked her what she wanted to do and when she announced she wanted to attend the jazz fest at the fairgrounds, he immediately asked what was in it for him and when she'd said nothing, he'd told her that was not the sort of people they should be associating with. She'd ended up not going, but in the back of her mind she'd been resentful and then felt guilty for feeling that way.

Her mother agreed to watch Maya despite a catty remark about Miss E., which Lydia ignored. And now she anxiously waited for Hunter while her mother sat on the sofa watching her.

"No etiquette lessons, Mother, no talk about proper behavior or acting like a lady," Lydia said. "Maya is just a child and I want her to be a child."

"What will we do while you're on your…date?"

"Watch a movie, play a game with her. She loves Monopoly."

Caroline looked doubtful. "But…"

"Mother, just enjoy your granddaughter. She will grow up soon enough."

A knock sounded on the door. Lydia opened it to find Hunter standing almost awkwardly in the hall. He looked so handsome, so distinguished. For a moment she felt like she was still in high school. He was dressed casually in dark brown pants and a jacket with a white shirt open at the neck.

"Ready?" he asked.

She nodded and waved goodbye to her mother and Maya, who had come out of her bedroom to grin happily at Lydia. "Have fun, Mom." She trotted over to her grandmother and plopped down on the floor.

The Cactus Flower Grill and Steak House looked like a log cabin with lots of wood beams and wood planking on the floor covered with peanut shells. The waitresses were dressed like Annie Oakley and the men were dressed like Roy Rodgers. Lydia was charmed by everything as the hostess showed her and Hunter to a booth. The booth was high backed, giving the illusion of privacy. Lydia settled on the comfortable cushion and glanced through the menu. The scent of steak and garlic made her mouth water.

"Tell me about what it's like to be an architect," she said after the waitress took their drink order. "And why did you decide to get into that field?"

"Blame it all on Lego." Hunter grinned at her happily. "I inherited my father's Lego collection when I was around six years old and the first thing I built was a skyscraper."

"How did you get into restoring old buildings? That's quite a leap from architect to preservationist."

"I want to preserve the past for the future. Our country has a history of just tearing things down and putting up new. I believe that if you have no idea where you came from, you have no idea where you're going."

"I understand that. But my parents and my husband had such different views. Even though my husband purchased the house his ancestors were slaves in, he did it to prove a point. By buying this house he somehow thought he was eliminating his origins, as though he was ashamed of where he came from." She paused for a second, marshaling her thoughts. Mitchell had avoided any mention of his family. Lydia had never understood why he felt such shame. "He didn't understand how important it was that we embrace the past and not destroy it. My ancestors, who survived in the bottom of leaky boats, left this incredible legacy to live up to. They had to be strong to survive that perilous passage and still thrive in a strange country."

"My ancestry is a little more convoluted," Hunter admitted. "I do understand what you mean about the past since

I make my living from it. My great-grandparents, Miss E.'s parents, moved from Nigeria to France and then to the United States. My grandfather was full-blooded Cherokee. I do understand what you're saying. The past dictates the future and we can't delete it as though it never happened."

"My parents think their past began when my father made his first million. Nothing else is important to them. The fact that my paternal grandmother took in laundry is something that is never spoken of. My father would have a stroke if he found out I knew about her."

"That's sad," Hunter said. "What about your mother?"

"I don't know much about her parents. My mother has always been very secretive about her background. They died when I was still a toddler. I know my parents love me, but I don't think they like me very much."

"That's because you're not what they expect you to be."

Lydia sighed. "In their eyes, I'm not bad daughter. I don't care for the conventions they take such pride in."

"Messing with their house of cards makes people nervous."

The waitress brought their drinks. Lydia took a sip of her merlot and smiled gratefully at the woman.

"When I met Miss E. I wanted her to be my grandmother. She is so unconventional and in such direct contrast to my parents."

Hunter grinned. "Yeah, she is. Makes you wonder how my siblings and I ended up in such conventional careers. You'd think one of us would have apprenticed with Miss E. Though Scott comes the closest to being unconventional."

"But he's in law enforcement."

"He is now. For a brief period of time he was doing things he couldn't talk about."

Lydia's curiosity was piqued. "Like what?" Scott seemed so reliable. Still waters ran deep with him.

"I don't know, he doesn't talk about it. Though we all have our suspicions."

The waitress returned for their food order. Hunter ordered rib eye and Lydia ordered shrimp. She mused over Hunter's comment about Scott. Had he been an assassin? A spy? A mercenary? He seemed so normal—a bit mysterious at times, but generally normal.

"What do your other siblings do?" Lydia had meant to ask Miss E. about the other grandchildren, but the timing had never been right.

"Donovan is a chef. He owns a restaurant in Paris. Kenzie is a fashion buyer for an upscale department store. She's in Milan right now. At least I think she is. She's not so good about checking in with Miss E. as the rest of us are."

"I wish I'd had brothers and sisters." Lydia didn't intend to sound so wistful.

"Some days having brothers and sisters is great," Hunter said, "and some days you just want the bathroom to yourself."

Lydia laughed at the idea of sharing a bathroom with brothers and sisters. She'd had her own private bathroom. Her parents each had their own bathrooms.

"I wanted someone to play with. My mother frowned on my playing with the servants' children even though there were several my age."

"Sounds lonely," Hunter said.

"It was." She looked back at all the times she'd sat in her window seat, watching the neighborhood kids riding their bikes up and down the sidewalks. She'd so wanted to join them.

"How did you keep yourself occupied?"

"I had an extensive imaginary world. I read every book I could lay my hands on." Some she'd even read over and over in them. "I loved *Alice's Adventures Through the*

Looking Glass, The Chronicles of Narnia, The Wizard of Oz."

"What about the Lord of the Rings trilogy?"

"No. It didn't have strong portrayals of women."

"So you're a fantasy reader."

She nodded. "I'll tell a secret."

He leaned forward, looking curious. "Do tell."

"The first year after Mitchell died, I thought about re-locating to San Diego. Maya and I went to look at properties and instead we ended up at Comic-Con. We even got dressed up in costume."

Hunter's eyebrows shot up. "You! At a comic book convention!"

"Yes." She remembered the thrill of the convention and the fun she and Maya had. Maya had been begging to return, but they missed it this year.

"One of my associates loves Comic-Con. She plans her entire vacation around the convention and starts working on her next costume the moment she gets back. One of her costumes took her six months to create."

Their food was delivered. Lydia breathed in the potent, savory scent of her shrimp.

"Since you told me your secret, I'll tell you mine." Hunter grinned boyishly at her.

She tilted her head. "You have a secret?"

"I wanted to be a pilot at one time, but I find flying model planes much more fun. If they crash nobody dies."

"Model planes!" Who knew, she thought. But then again, why not?

"It's cutthroat competition."

"How can flying a model plane be cutthroat?"

"We race. We have stunt-flying competitions. One club I belong to re-enacts famous air battles from different wars. In my alterego, I'm Daniel Chappy James, Jr. He was a Tuskegee pilot flying a P-51 Mustang during World War II." He looked like a little boy opening a Christmas gift and finding a puppy inside the box as he talked about flying model aircraft.

"I'm stunned and amazed." She could almost picture him in his uniform, his cap at a jaunty angle. Heat flared and she hoped it didn't reach her face.

"Well, I'm picturing you in a metal bikini like Princess Leia's."

"I used to dream I was Princess Leia with the whole future of the galaxy resting on my shoulders," she said.

"In a metal bikini?" he asked hopefully.

She laughed, shaking her head. "No, just with the cinnamon buns on the sides of my head." He was flirting with her and she felt empowered. Mitchell never flirted with her. Though David and Leon had made passes at her, but she'd given them such a cold reaction they'd never done so again. Thinking about then cast a shadow over her. She struggled to put them back in their box, not wanting them to dim the delightful time she was having with Hunter.

"Who knew the two of us could have such rich, lavish fantasy lives." He took her hand and held her fingers tight in his.

A shiver of something so strong shook Lydia.

Their food came and silence fell over them as they each experimented with their food. Lydia's shrimp was delicious. And from the satisfied look on Hunter's face, his steak was just as good.

Somewhere in the bar, someone tuned a guitar and did a sound check on the mic. Lydia tilted her head to listen. Country music wasn't her favorite, but she could tolerate it. Now give her a good jazz band any time and she was transported.

"What do you want?" Hunter asked suddenly. He put his knife and fork down.

No one had ever asked her what she wanted before. Always her worth was wrapped around what other people wanted from her. "I wanted an adventure. Something spontaneous that wasn't programmed into Mitchell's two-year calendar schedule. I don't want to get approval for a dress I want to wear to make sure it's the right kind of dress for the right kind of occasion. I want to wear my favorite one whenever I chose to." Mitchell had coded her closet and had his assistant label each dress, when it had been worn and who had seen her in it. All Lydia could think about at the time was what a waste of the assistant's time.

"So moving to Reno, winning a hotel/casino and buying a house wasn't enough of an adventure for you?"

"Maybe next year I want to sail down the Amazon and not have to make sure it fits into my calendar." Thinking about it, her life had been stifling. She had been in service to her father's and Mitchell's ambitions and hadn't known how stifling it was until she'd thrown off the yoke and come to Reno. Just the thought of being forced back, caving in to her father's demands made her furious.

They finished their food to the music blasting from the bar. Lydia's thoughts whirled. She didn't want to think about David and Leon and the coming custody battle. She wanted to have faith in the justice system, but little doubts nagged her. She tensed up, her fingers tightening around the stem of her wineglass so tightly she had to force herself to release it, worried she'd break it.

"Let's get out of here," Hunter said once the bill was paid. He rose and held out a hand to her.

"Where are we going?"

"Let's take a walk. We have time before the concert in

the park. You need to relax and stop thinking about your father, your mother, David, Leon, the casino, the future."

"But the future—" she said.

"The future is going to happen no matter what plans you make."

She placed her hand in his and let him draw her to her feet. Moments later, the valet delivered his Mercedes and they were driving back to the hotel.

Instead of parking in his usual spot, Hunter drove to the very back of the lot and parked next to a path that led to the hot springs.

"What—?" she started to ask.

"Shh," Hunter replied, placing his fingers on her mouth. He took her hand and led her down the path, skirting the perimeter of the hotel and out into the desert until the music and laughter fell away into silence.

The quarter moon cast gray shadows over the landscape. The path was lit by tiny solar lights that cast just enough light to show them the path, but nothing else. Lydia heard rustlings in the underbrush. Overhead a shadow, wings outstretched, cruised the perimeter of the hot springs. Did hawks hunt at night? Or was it an owl?

Lydia shivered. Unlike Louisiana, where the heat and humidity hung heavy in the air day and night, Reno cooled down. She took a deep breath, pulling the cooler night air into her lungs.

"Want to go skinny-dipping?"

"What?"

The darkness hid her facial expression, but Hunter could almost picture her shock. "You and me in the water."

There was a long pause.

"Yes," she said quietly.

"Really?" Did he really just say that?

"You thought I would say no?"

He did. "Of course not."

Lydia quickly undressed, peeling her clothes off one piece at a time, and walked into the water. He was so stunned he couldn't seem to move. She was as beautiful as he'd imagined.

She turned around and looked at him; her hands were covering her breasts. "Are you coming in?"

"Yeah."

"If you don't want to…"

He liked this bold woman. She was so sexy, so stunning, so unexpected. He quickly undressed and joined her in the water. Lydia had swum out to the center of the hot springs. She watched him as he glided toward her. She turned to him and Hunter ran his hands up Lydia's arms. He kept waiting for her to say no, but she didn't. He leaned over and kissed her. Her mouth was soft, yielding. She tasted sweet like the wine from dinner. "I want you."

He wanted her too. From the first moment he had seen her looking so fragile and vulnerable, he knew he wanted this woman with a passion he'd never felt before. "I know."

"Are you scared?"

"No."

He lifted an eyebrow. He didn't really believe her.

The water lapped around them. They floated for a bit, the moon lighting the water. Lydia eased back toward the shallows. When his feet touched the bottom, he turned and pulled her toward him. Her breasts pressed into his chest, she felt so soft. Part of him knew this could turn into a mistake of monumental portions, but hell if he cared. Her nails dug into his back.

"Make love to me, Hunter." Her voice had a breathless quality to it.

Slowly he lifted her up and she wrapped her legs around his waist. She felt so delicate and fragile. "Lydia."

"Stop talking." Her lips found his.

He thrust up into her and her heat enveloped him. He bit his bottom lip to stop from crying out. She wriggled against him, her legs firmly clasped around his waist. He moved slowly wanting to savor every moment. The water lapped gently against their bodies.

How he loved the feel of her silken skin against him, the tautness of her breasts, the sweetness of her breath. He'd never forget this moment as long as he lived.

He increased his pace driving up into her, their bodies becoming one. She devoured his mouth and her passion overwhelmed him. Her body began to shake and he knew she was close.

"Hunter, Hunter," she chanted in a sensual whisper over and over again.

He closed his eyes and gave one final thrust. Lydia groaned as her muscles gripped him in a tight spasm.

Dear God, he wanted this woman like he'd never wanted another. And in that moment he made himself a promise. He would do anything he had to do to protect her.

Chapter 11

Lydia felt awkward around Hunter. The memory of their lovemaking the night before left her feeling hot and breathless. They both leaned against a fence watching as her new neighbor, Hector Ibarra, showed Maya the horse she would begin her training on.

She cast a side glance at Hunter. He seemed so unconcerned with what had happened between them, yet she sensed a watchful tenseness in him. When he looked at her, she grew even more hot and flustered even though she felt very comfortable with him. She'd never felt comfortable with a lot of men, not even Mitchell. Mitchell had intimidated her. Hunter didn't.

"What do you think?" Hunter asked, gesturing at the horse.

"What do I know about horses, except they're big and unpredictable?" And they bite.

His arm brushed hers. A spike of heat jolted her. He was only the second man she'd ever slept with and the memory of their lovemaking at the hot springs made her tingle all over in a way Mitchell had never done for her. She wanted to grab him and kiss him. She wanted to feel his hands on her, stroking her skin, bringing her pleasure in a way she'd never felt with Mitchell. She wanted more.

"From what I understand, they're basically big dogs," Hunter replied.

Hector helped Maya mount a pinto horse that looked way too big for such a little girl. She squealed in delight. Hector's daughter, Patti, mounted on her own horse, grinned at Maya.

"Dogs bite," Lydia said.

"You have to let the little bird leave the nest."

Lydia shook her head. "Spoken by the man who doesn't have a little bird in the nest."

"I have you." He turned his gaze on her and reached out to push a strand of hair out of her eyes.

Lydia leaned into the intimacy of his caress. Sex with Mitchell had been predictable, but nice. He had made sure she enjoyed it as much as he had. Sex with Hunter was explosive and passionate, making her body long for even more. Everything she thought sex was supposed to be. Just the memory sent spirals of heat through her. Hunter leaned over and kissed her on the lips.

"Mama," Maya called. "Look at me. I'm—" Her voice trailed away as she trotted her horse to the other side of the huge corral.

Hector walked over to them. "What do you think?"

"I don't know what to think," Lydia said. "It's not like buying shoes."

"Sure it is," Hector said with a bellowing laugh. "Your daughter is smart, a little hyper,active and logical. Cupcake is steady as a rock. She's a great beginner horse. Maya and Cupcake could grow together."

"How do you know?" Cupcake! Who named a horse Cupcake? Lydia had visions of pink frosting swirled over tiny cupcakes.

Hector grinned. "I've been matching little girls with

horses for over thirty years. Those two are going to go together like bacon and eggs."

"Mama," Maya said, pulling the horse gently to a stop in front of Lydia. "I want Cupcake. Please. She's the one."

"But you've only looked at a couple of horses."

Maya patted Cupcake's neck. "Cupcake is perfect." She bent over and put her arms around the animal's neck. "I love her."

Hector's grin grew. Hunter patted the horse's head. Its ears twitched back and forth.

"I guess I'm out-voted," Lydia said. She tentatively patted the horse's soft nose and was surprised at the velvety smoothness. She looked into the dark brown eyes and saw nothing but gentleness. Cupcake was indeed perfect and Maya would love her.

"Okay, let's do it."

"Until you get your stable up and running," Hector said, "I'll board her. I won't let her go until Maya is capable of taking care of Cupcake by herself."

"You need to learn to ride, too, Mama," Maya said.

"I do?" Lydia wasn't certain she wanted to learn anymore. As a child, she'd been wild to have a horse, but she'd given up that dream when she realized her parents would never allow it.

"Yes." Maya nodded her head emphatically. "Mr. Ibarra can find a horse for you, too."

Lydia shook her head. Just the idea frightened her a little. "I don't think so."

Hector laughed. "I've got the perfect horse for you. Come on into the barn and meet Misty."

Lydia shook her head again, but Hunter grabbed her arm and propelled her toward the open doors of the barn.

The barn was divided into three parts. Down the center ran a long aisle bordered on either side by open stalls.

The area near the doors contained tack neatly hanging from hooks on the wall. Saddles were tossed over large sawhorse-like forms.

Hector led Lydia down the wide aisle to a stall. A head poked over the door and Lydia's breath caught in her throat.

"Say hello to Misty," Hector said.

"Go on," Hunter urged her. "Pet her."

Lydia simply stared. The horse regarded her patiently. She was a pretty horse with wide brown eyes and a mottled gray coat. A grayish-white mane hung from her neck. She shook her head and the mane went flying.

Lydia tried not to panic when Hector slipped a halter over the horse's head and opened the stall. He led Misty out into the aisle and tied the halter to a ring in a post. In seconds Hector saddled the horse.

"I'm not really dressed for riding." Lydia glanced down at her jeans and sneakers.

"You're wearing pants," Hunter said. "You're fine."

Once saddled and a bit slipped into her mouth, Hector led Misty to a block in the yard with steps leading up.

Lydia shook nervously. She wasn't getting on that horse. It was so big.

"We'll all learn to ride." Hunter helped Lydia onto the mounting block. He nodded at Hector, who looked at him up and down critically.

"I don't have anything for you," Hector said, "but I know just the horse. He's a gelding I saw at a friend's place. I'm pretty sure Sultan is for sale. I'll check into it."

Hector showed Lydia where to place her feet. "I'll lead you and Misty around the yard."

Once she was in the saddle and the stirrups adjusted for her, Hector placed her feet properly in the stirrups even though she wore the wrong shoes and then walked the horse around the yard while Lydia clung for dear life.

Not that the horse was going to bolt with Hector holding the reins.

"That's it, Mom," Maya called. "Isn't it wonderful? This is going to be so much fun."

"I have to think about this." Lydia hung on to the saddle horn, her legs tightly gripping the horse's body.

"We can do this together," Maya said and giggled.

After a few minutes under Hector's gentle instruction, she started to relax. She suddenly understood what Maya felt. Riding a horse was wonderful even though she was somewhat terrified. The ground was a long way down though and she eyed it with trepidation. What if Misty did something and tossed Lydia off? She tried not to think how far she would fall.

Hunter leaned against the fence, arms resting on the top pole. He watched her, his eyes alight with amusement. "You go, Lydia," he called as she passed him.

This was not what Lydia had in mind. The idea of learning to ride was terrifying.

Didn't she want an adventure? a little voice whispered in her ear. Here was another adventure for her to experience. Suddenly, the shackles of her childhood melted and dropped away. Why not? she asked herself, sitting up a bit straighter. Isn't this why she'd left New Orleans? Isn't this why she wanted to buy a house, to own a hotel and casino? Her gaze fell on Hunter. Isn't this why she was falling in love with Hunter?

Lydia wrote a check for the horses and arranged for room and board with Hector for the time being. Hunter drove Lydia back to the hotel. Hector and Patti had asked if Maya could spend the rest of the afternoon with them learning to take care of her horse and getting a few more lessons in on riding. At first Lydia had been reluctant, but Hunter pointed out they could leave the security team

Scott had assigned to Maya. They were diligent and discreet. Lydia knew the two men had fallen under Maya's
spell, too, even though they worked hard to hide it. She
kissed Maya goodbye and drove back to the Mariposa
with Hunter.

The casino was filled to capacity. Lydia stood in the
doorway watching the flashing lights and listening to the
chimes. Maya had been turned over to her tutor. School
started in a few weeks and she needed to be ready. The
tutor had been optimistic that Maya would adjust well, yet
Lydia still worried. Education was important. Even though
her parents had groomed her to be a trophy wife, they had
still insisted on a good education. Lydia wasn't certain
what a degree in Elizabethan culture would ever do for her.

A woman, dressed in black pants and white shirt, approached Lydia. Her name was engraved on a tag that
adorned her white shirt. Alice Porter was the pit boss at
the blackjack tables.

"Ms. Montgomery, can I have a moment of your time?
In private"

Lydia smiled. "Let's go to my office." Lydia led the
way to the administrative area behind the check-in counter. Once in her office, she waited for Alison to enter and
then closed the door.

Alice's face was drawn into deep worry lines. Though
she appeared calm, she clenched and unclenched her hands.
She took a deep breath. "I need to talk to you about something."

"Is everything okay, Alice?"

"I don't know how to tell you this," Alice said.

"Just say it," Lydia said kindly, trying not to envision
all the things that could go wrong in the casino.

"Your father is losing a lot of money at the blackjack tables."

"My father is gambling?" Lydia couldn't contain her surprise.

Alice nodded. "Jasper used to cover certain people, usually family members, and when your father identified himself as your father, I extended the privilege to him." Her voice trailed away.

"But—" Lydia coaxed.

"He may be a family member, but we still have a limit and he's getting ready to cross it. He's lost nearly $250,000 dollars. When I asked him about it, he said you would cover his losses."

"Me," Lydia said, frowning, uncertain how to respond. "Thank you. Please inform the dealers that the bank of Lydia is closed. When he gives you a problem, you can direct him to me. I will handle the situation."

Alice said thanks and left. Lydia sat down behind her desk and waited. As she waited for her father to make his appearance, anger rose in her. How arrogant of her father to expect her to cover his losses. He should be covering his own losses.

The door to her office flung open and bounced against the wall. Her father stalked in, eyes narrowed, mouth pinched in fury. Andrew slammed the door closed. "How dare you embarrass me in front of the entire casino."

"Sit down." Lydia pointed at a chair. She glared at her father. "How dare you embarrass me?"

"I am your father and you will not speak to me in that manner."

Lydia took a deep breath, preparing herself for the battle. She rested her hands calmly on the top of her desk. "I'm a businessperson, and you may be my father, but that doesn't give you the right to play fast and loose with my business."

"Right," he sneered. "Owning a casino is beneath us."

"Losing $250,000 is hardly a social coup."

"If you had stayed where you belonged, I wouldn't be here."

Lydia frowned. "I beg your pardon."

He scowled at her. "If you'd stayed in New Orleans and funded my campaign—"

"What makes you think I would want you to be mayor of New Orleans?"

He gaped at her. "You ungrateful little brat. After everything I've done for you. If I hadn't brokered a deal with Mitchell for you, you'd be—"

Shocked, Lydia stared at the man who was her father. "You sold me to Mitchell?"

"I traded you for that piece of land on the outskirts of New Orleans I wanted to develop."

Lydia jumped to her feet, shaken by his revelation. "You what?"

"You heard me." He sat back in the chair, arms crossed over his chest, a smug look on his face. "If not for me, you wouldn't be such a wealthy widow."

"Get out," Lydia said calmly.

"Excuse me?"

"Get out," she repeated, her voice rising. She walked to the door and opened it. "Get out."

Andrew shrugged, stood and walked toward her. "Baby, don't be hasty. You know I love you."

Lydia closed her eyes and pointed at the door. After her father left, she collapsed against it, sliding down to sit on the floor, tears falling down her cheeks. Her marriage had been nothing but a travesty. A real estate deal. Her mind flooded with images of Mitchell taking her to business dinners and fund-raisers. He'd been attentive, but they'd only been alone a few times during the months of their engagement. He'd showered her with expensive gifts and flowers, and she'd been flattered, thinking the gifts meant he was fond of her. Had all those actions just been one big lie? Had he ever really loved her? How naïve had she been?

She pushed herself to her feet, wiped the tears away while wrestling with one final thought. Was her father lying to hurt her because he was mad, or were his words the truth? She had to find her mother and ask.

Lydia found her mother in her suite removing clothes from a dozen shopping bags.

"What's on your mind, Lydia?" Caroline said as she held a black dress up to her and studied herself in the mirror over the fireplace.

"Did you know Dad's been gambling up a storm and expects me to cover his losses?"

"What's the problem with that? You own the casino; we should be able to use it."

"I'm not covering his losses," Lydia said.

Caroline dropped the black silk dress and whirled around. "What do you mean you're not covering his losses?"

"Just what I said. I'm not covering Dad's losses."

A look of panic crossed Caroline's face. She bent to pick up the dress and flung it over the back of a chair. "You have to."

"No, I do not."

"You have to," Caroline said.

"Give me one good reason," Lydia said.

"If you don't, we'll have to declare bankruptcy."

Lydia sat down, her legs no longer able to hold her. "What?" Had she heard correctly?

"The last development your dad managed fell through

when the bottom dropped out of the real estate market. We lost almost half our portfolio. And then…" Caroline opened another shopping bag and drew out a pair of white linen pants. She held them up and gently placed them over the back of the sofa.

"And then…" Lydia prompted.

"Well, Leon and David were so nice about it."

"About what?" Lydia's eyes narrowed. She felt like she was watching a newscast with the words "More disastrous news to come. Watch at eleven."

"They told Andrew he could borrow whatever he needed to get back on his feet." Caroline sat down, her knees pressed tightly together and her hands clenching and unclenching.

Bits and pieces of information dropped into place in Lydia's mind. "So that's why you and Dad sided with Leon and David over Maya. You owe them money. How much money do you owe them?"

Caroline hesitated.

"How much money do you owe them?" Lydia pressed her mother harder.

"Four and half million," Caroline whispered. "They promised if we could help them get control of Maya, they would forgive the loan."

Lydia felt like she was hyperventilating. She pressed trembling fingers to her hot cheeks. She stood. "I can't talk to you right now." She turned for the door.

"Lydia," Caroline pleaded. "Don't go away angry. Your father did what he thought was best."

Lydia stopped with one hand on the doorknob. She glanced back at her mother. "Best for whom?" Certainly not best for Maya or Lydia. She realized that her father considered what was best for himself first and then insisted it was best for everybody.

* * *

Hunter dropped his briefcase on his desk. The coffee-maker in the corner spit out coffee. After a morning at the building department to work out any kinks they had before issuing building permits had left him mildly annoyed.

He poured himself a cup and went back to his desk. Coffee was his savior. He sipped it as he looked over the building permit. They could start construction of the spa on Monday. He had the contractor already in place and ready to go.

Lydia appeared in the doorframe, an urgent look on her face. "Do you have a minute?"

"I've got maybe ten."

She shrugged her shoulders. "This is more than ten minutes' worth of sharing. I'll come back later."

"Whoa. I can spare as much time as you need." He gestured at the only empty chair in his office. Somehow he'd managed to fill every flat surface with files, blueprints and other assorted minutiae that seemed to be part of the life of an architect.

Lydia sat down. "My parents sold me to my husband."

"I thought that was illegal."

Her eyes shone with unshed tears even as her mouth twisted with hurt anger. "Apparently not." She brushed the wetness from her eyes as she went on explaining the convoluted story until Hunter started to feel furious for her. By the time she ended up with her father's debt, Hunter's hand hovered over the phone. He was prepared to call Scott to have them all thrown out of the hotel.

"And now they want to sell my daughter to Leon and David." Lydia jumped to her feet. She moved restlessly about the room, stopping at the table holding the facsimile of the spa. She explained about the debt her father had incurred.

"Just say the word and we'll have Scott remove them. There is a sign in the lobby that states we have the right to refuse service. We can have them gone in twenty minutes."

"You have no idea how tempted I am."

"What's stopping you?"

"You know and I know we need to keep them here under observation."

"But are they worth the turmoil?"

"To stop them from maybe taking my daughter? Yes. Considering how low they've gone, I think there are still lower levels unknown."

"Why don't you go on up to your suite, calm down and relax. I'll get Scott and we'll plan your next move."

"I'll call Vanessa and find out where we are on the DNA sample from Mitchell." With a plan in place, Lydia left and Hunter reached for the phone to fill Scott in on the newest development.

Lydia walked down the hall to her suite with dragging footsteps. So much had happened to send her down so many different emotional paths, she knew she needed time alone. Thankfully, Maya was with Hector and his daughter, but they would be bringing her home within the hour. Lydia decided she had just enough time for a long, soothing bath.

She opened the door to her suite. As anxious as she was to be in her own home, she felt the suite had become a second home for her. She'd come to like the texture of the rooms and the vibrant Spanish colors.

Before she could head to the bathroom to start a bath, a knock sounded on the door. She opened it to find Leon and David standing out in the hall.

"Can we come in?" Leon said. "We really need to talk to you."

"Why?"

"It's about Maya."

"Are you giving up your custody battle?"

He pulled a small gun from his pocket and gestured for her to back up. "No."

Lydia stumbled backward. "What are you doing?" *Don't panic. Don't panic. Don't panic.*

"Where's Maya?"

"You come in here with a gun demanding to know where my daughter is. I don't think so."

"Then we'll wait. She's bound to show up sometime. David," Leon ordered, "go into Maya's bedroom and pack some overnight clothes."

"You're kidnapping her!"

"No," Leon replied, pulling a piece of paper out of his jacket pocket, "you're signing over custody of her." He thrust the paper at Lydia. "Sign it."

She refused to take the paper, but Leon thrust the gun in her face. "Sign it."

Lydia took the paper, unfolded it and sat down on the sofa. "I have to read it first."

"Lydia, just sign it." Leon waved the gun at her.

"Do you have a pen?"

Leon stared at her and then reached inside his jacket pocket again. "Read it and then sign it and stop procrastinating."

"You know a contract signed under duress isn't binding." She set the paper down on the coffee table and smoothed it out.

"I'll have possession of Maya and isn't possession nine tenths of the law?"

For a second fear slithered her through her. She smoothed the creased paper again and started reading.

In the back of her mind, she hoped Hunter found Scott quickly.

She read it through twice. The custody transfer was a boilerplate Leon had printed from some website. From Maya's bedroom she could hear drawers opening and closing. David muttered and Leon walked to the bedroom door to look inside while still keeping the gun trained on her.

Lydia considered flight, but Leon would catch her before she was close enough to the door to escape. *Hurry up, Hunter,* she prayed, pushing the panic down again. She needed to keep her head.

"Lydia," Leon said, an edge of warning in his tone. "Sign it."

She read through the document one more time and picked up the pen. "If I don't?"

"I'm holding a gun, Lydia."

"But if you shoot me someone will hear and investigate." *Keep them talking,* she thought. Hunter and Scott should be here any minute.

"These rooms are sound-proof. Now sign the damn thing or I'll break every one of your pretty little fingers. Then they won't be so pretty anymore."

As if she cared. She would die for Maya. She didn't think Leon could break them all at once, though the pain could be a deterrent. "Oh, what to do? What to do?"

Leon frowned at her. Lydia picked up the pen. An idea had just occurred to her. She smiled as she scribbled Lydia M. Mouse at the bottom of the paper. She put the pen down, refolded the paper carefully so he wouldn't see what she'd written and left it sitting on the table with the pen neatly lined up with it.

Leon grinned in triumph, picked up the folded paper and thrust it into his pocket. "David, what's taking so long in there?"

"I'm coming," David yelled back.

Lydia saw a shadow on the patio. She watched the shadow out of the corner of her eyes. Suddenly Scott's face peered in quickly and disappeared again.

"Why do you want Maya so badly?" Lydia asked. "I control her inheritance. I can write you a check today for any amount you want."

"I want everything."

Now that she'd signed the paper, Lydia could see that Leon wanted to be friendly.

"Why just ask for a pie when I can have the whole bakery?"

"What do you think Maya is going to say in ten years and when she's eighteen and discovered you've pretty much plundered her estate?"

Leon shrugged. "Do I care? Six hundred fifty million will go a long way. When that's gone, I'll break up the investment company and parcel it off. Be happy I'm not asking for your money."

"Why is the money so important? Mitchell left you fifty million dollars."

"Because that little brat took everything," Leon snarled. "Once she came along my father didn't have time for us anymore."

"Maybe the problem wasn't Mitchell but you. You fathered two children and abandoned them. You refused to take responsibility for your children as their father. You screwed up every job your father gave you."

"I didn't want to work in the mailroom."

Lydia sighed. "Your job was to learn how the company worked from the bottom up."

Scott had opened the patio door and stepped into the dining area. He moved soundlessly across the floor and into Maya's bedroom.

"That company was mine by right." Leon waved the gun at her, his face set with anger.

"You've never earned anything."

"Like you have, Miss Trophy Wife," he sneered.

"I'm a good parent." And she had earned the right to raise her daughter in the best way she saw fit, which included learning to ride to make her daughter happy.

A knock sounded on the door to the suite.

"Don't answer it," Leon growled.

"If I don't answer it, people are going to be concerned and call security. I'll just get rid of them." She heard a muffled sound from Maya's bedroom. Scott poked his head out and then back inside again.

Lydia walked calmly to the door. Leon followed her, the gun pressed against her spine, his attention wholly on her. A knock sounded again. Lydia opened the door to find Hunter standing there.

"Lydia, got a minute?"

"I do."

"She doesn't," Leon said. "We're in the middle of something."

"Really." Hunter pointed at something behind Leon. "Maybe you need to talk to my brother."

In the next second, Leon was whirled around and neatly disarmed by Scott. Hunter grabbed Lydia and pulled her out of the way. Leon fell to the floor writhing in pain with Scott standing over him, the small gun now in his hand.

"That was too easy." Scott sounded disappointed. He looked at the gun, ejected the clip and then put the gun in one pocket and the clip in another. He grabbed Leon by the arm and jerked him to his feet while smoothly sliding handcuffs on his wrists.

Chapter 12

"You can't have us arrested," Leon protested as two uniformed police officers and two detectives stood in Lydia's suite. "We're now Maya's legal guardians. Think of the scandal."

"About that." Lydia asked the police detective to retrieve the folded paper from Leon's jacket pocket and handed it to Lydia. She opened the paper and held it up in front of Leon's face. "Lydia M. Mouse has no legal authority to sign this piece of trumped up custody contract. Especially under duress." She handed the paper back to the detective, who dropped it into a paper envelope.

Vanessa Peabody entered the suite, a curious look on her face. She held her briefcase in one hand. "What's going on?"

"We're just in the middle of a little hostage situation," Lydia said.

"I demand to see my lawyer," Leon yelled.

"He's five minutes behind me," Vanessa said. She opened her briefcase and pulled out an envelope. "I have good news and I have better news." She smiled at the detective. "Could you wait a moment before taking them away?"

The lead detective nodded. A few moments later, Leon and David's lawyer, Kramer O'Reilly, entered. "What the hell is going on here?"

Leon surged forward but was stopped by the tight grip the police officer had on his arm. "Make these goons release me."

Kramer half smiled. "I need to know what's going on."

Lydia stepped forward. "Leon and David tried to force me to sign a bogus custody paper for my daughter."

"Did you sign it?" Vanessa asked frowning.

"Not with my real name," Lydia said with a tight grin. She nodded at the detective, who opened the envelope and allowed Vanessa and Kramer to glance at it before returning it to the envelope.

"Smart girl," Vanessa said.

"I have my moments." Lydia sat down. "So what's the good news?"

Vanessa grinned. "The good news is that Maya is definitely your husband's daughter."

"Should that be the better news?" Hunter asked curiously.

"The better news is…" Vanessa glanced at Leon and David, who leaned forward to look at her. "The better news is that Leon and David are not your late husband's sons." She handed a piece of paper to Lydia.

Lydia glanced through the paper. "Oh my."

"That's a lie," Leon said.

Kramer O'Reilly took the paper and glanced through it.

"And," Vanessa grinned wider, "better news, part two." She whipped out another paper from her briefcase. "I spoke with Mitchell's lawyer and Mr. Tynan faxed me this letter." She handed it to Lydia. "Mitchell knew Leon and David weren't his sons, but…" she glanced at them "…he chose to provide for them anyway."

"That's not true," David cried.

Lydia read the letter from Mitchell's lawyer, Everest Tynan. The prose was dry and filled with legalese, but the gist was Mitchell knew very well that neither Leon nor David were his biological children. Lydia couldn't help the feeling of sadness filling her.

Kramer took the letter from Lydia and glanced through it. "It looks pretty true to me and the DNA results definitely show that you have no familial relationship with the man who raised you."

"No," David said, shaking his head. "No."

"Are you going to press charges?" the lead detective asked. "They did threaten you with a gun."

Lydia was very tempted to say yes. These two men had threatened to hurt her. She wanted to punish them for making her so afraid, for making her life miserable, for making her parents threaten her. But she couldn't. She looked at Hunter, who shook his head slightly. He knew what she needed to do.

"I'm not pressing charges," Lydia said quietly.

Leon and David were released. The police left. Lydia sat down on the sofa feeling drained.

Scott had his own security people in the suite in seconds. "You have thirty minutes to pack, settle your bill and get out of here. My people will escort you to your suite and then out of this hotel."

Leon and his brother looked totally defeated.

"Just get them out of here," Lydia said. "I'll take care of their bill."

"Lydia," Hunter said.

"Its okay, Hunter." She pointed at the door. "Get out. If you aren't out of Nevada within twenty-four hours, I will be contacting this very nice detective—" she held up his business card "—and re-instating my complaint. And Scott here will personally take you to the airport and make sure you leave. Don't come back to Nevada."

"If you come back," Vanessa put in, "Lydia can still

file her complaint. It's to your interest to stay as far away from Nevada as you possibly can, and never come back."

Leon glared at Lydia. "This isn't over."

"Yes, it is," Hunter said firmly.

Scott herded the two men to the door and pushed them out. Two of his security people fell into step behind them with Scott in the rear. Leon looked furious. David looked defeated. Lydia simply felt sorry for them.

"I guess I have no legal reason to be here," Kramer said. He picked up his briefcase and left, leaving Lydia, Hunter and Vanessa alone.

"Who knew?" Lydia headed to the kitchen. She was desperately in need of coffee.

"Apparently not them," Vanessa said, following.

Hunter sat on the sofa rereading the DNA results and the letter from Everest Tynan.

Later they sat around the coffee table.

"You knew, didn't you?" Lydia asked Vanessa as she sipped her coffee.

"I suspected," Vanessa said. "When the results showed no familial relationship between Maya and the brothers, I contacted Mr. Tynan to find out if he knew anything. He had the letter, but we both decided DNA results would be more conclusive."

"I feel sorry for them," Lydia said. "They loved Mitchell. They thought he was their father. If it were me, I'd be devastated."

Hunter shrugged. "I think what is even more stunning is that Mitchell took care of them even though he knew."

Lydia thought about Mitchell. She'd just discovered a side of him she hadn't known. She knew he'd loved David and Leon, but their behavior had upset him. He could have told them at any time, but he didn't. Even when he was dying of cancer he'd kept the secret.

A knock sounded at the door. Lydia opened it to find Scott standing there.

"How did it go?" Lydia asked as she walked back to the sofa. She poured Scott a cup of coffee and handed it to him.

Scott took a deep breath. "I felt sorry for them. David is more upset than Leon. He was crying while he packed."

"Really," Hunter said. "I've never known you to feel almost sorry for someone."

Scott shrugged. "I don't think they ever once entertained the thought that they might be the ones who weren't Mitchell's biological sons."

Lydia said nothing. Mitchell had provided for them when he didn't have to and he still acknowledged them. She was sad that she never got to know that part of him despite being married to him for seven years. How could she not have known?

"I think you should know," Scott said. "David and Leon have pretty much frittered away their inheritance. If they don't take control, they're going to be looking for jobs soon. Both of them made a few bad investments."

Of which one of them was lending money to her father. Maybe she wasn't going to be rid of them. If Mitchell still felt responsible for them, was she still responsible, as well? She would have to think long and hard. Though her dad did owe them a considerable sum. She would probably have to pony up and pay it, but not right away.

"I'd best be going," Scott said. He pushed out of the chair, drained the last of his coffee and walked to the door. A knock sounded just as he twisted the knob.

Caroline Fairchild stood in the hall. She looked tired and worried with a lot of panic in her eyes. Scott stood aside after a short nod from Lydia to let her mother in. He closed the door after him, leaving Lydia and Hunter alone with Caroline.

"Lydia, what have you done?" Caroline cried as she rushed into the living room.

"What do you mean?"

Tears gathered in her eyes. "We're ruined. Your dad and I are ruined. Leon called in the loan payable immediately. We're going to lose our home, our reputation, our social standing. What did you do?"

"She didn't do anything," Hunter said in Lydia's defense. "She protected herself when Leon and David threatened her. With a gun."

A shocked look showed on Caroline's face. Lydia tried to push aside the hurt that filled her. Her mother was putting the burden of her father's mismanagement on Lydia's shoulders. Her father was a grown adult. Caroline should be blaming him.

"Sit down, Mom," Lydia said. She went to the kitchen to pour a cup of coffee for her mother and handed her a mug,

Caroline covered her face with her hands, harsh sobs starting. "We're ruined."

Lydia's first thought was to immediately pay off Leon and David, but she didn't want to. Her parents had sided with them against her. What did she owe them? She knew she was being childish, yet she couldn't ignore the feelings of hurt and betrayal. Yet they were Maya's grandparents and they did love her.

"I didn't make this mess," Lydia said, "but I will help you out of this for Maya's sake."

"I can tell Leon you'll pay him the money as soon as possible." Caroline looked relieved.

"I'm not paying the loan. You're responsible for the loan and Leon has every expectation you will repay it." If she did, Lydia's father would feel like he could borrow any amount he wanted because he knew she'd get him out of his hole.

"Lydia," Caroline cried out, a stricken look on her face. "You would let us be homeless."

Lydia wanted to feel sorry for her mother, but didn't. "You won't be homeless." If she had to, Lydia would let them live in Mitchell's home. "I'll arrange for you and Dad to talk to Collier Preston. He's a financial consultant who is on staff in Earnest Tynan's office. He'll help you the same way he helped me." Mitchell had been a realist, knowing Lydia would outlive him. He'd arranged for Lydia to have Preston teach her how to manage her money and how to find the right investments. Mitchell might not have cared much about Lydia's desire to own a casino/hotel, but he trusted her to make good financial decisions.

"You won't help us," Caroline cried.

"I am helping you. I'm helping you to help yourselves."

Her mother's face crumpled and she started to sob so heart-wrenchingly, Lydia almost changed her mind.

"Mrs. Fairchild." Hunter handed her a tissue. "You're the parent here. You're supposed to be looking out for Lydia's interests."

Caroline mopped up her tears. The tissue came away stained with mascara and eyeshadow. "Who are you to speak to me this way?"

"I'm the man who loves your daughter and your granddaughter."

Lydia glanced at him, startled. He'd said the *love* word. "Hunter!"

"Sorry. I didn't want to tell you this way, but it seemed the right thing to say."

Lydia beamed at him. She'd resisted the idea of being in love with him for so long that all her defenses fell away. "I love you, too. We'll talk about this later."

He grinned. "I know."

She felt a golden glow fill her. She turned to her mother

and reached out to hold her hand. "This has to stop. You cannot move people around on a chess board for your own needs. I can either help you in the short term, or in the long term. Because I love you, I'm choosing to help you in the long run." She picked up a clean tissue and cleaned the smudge of makeup from her mother's cheeks. "I'm going to talk to Leon and David and ask them to give you more time to pay off the loan. I'm sure they'll be happy to do so." Lydia had no problem informing them of the alternatives she had in mind if they didn't agree. She was certain they would be happy to extend the loan in the face of some jail time.

"And then what?" Caroline asked harshly.

"Dad didn't need me to make his first million. He can do it again." She bit the inside of her lip before saying the next part. "Reno is booming. There are a lot of opportunities for investment here. I think maybe you and Dad need a change." She glanced at Hunter, who cringed. "And," Lydia continued, "with your ability to socialize, you and Dad will be back on top in no time. If Reno isn't to your satisfaction, Seattle is booming. Or San Francisco. You and Dad need to think outside the box."

Caroline's sobs drained away. She studied her daughter. "Why would we want to leave New Orleans?"

"Why stay? I think you need a fresh perspective."

Her mother sat back in the chair, contemplating Lydia's words. "I don't know if your father is going to like your idea."

"That's fine. I have things to wrap up here. I'll talk to him in a couple hours. I'm sure he'll listen to reason."

Caroline rose to her feet unsteadily and departed, her face a tragic mask of despair. Lydia felt sorry for her mother, but Hunter was right. Caroline and Andrew were the parents.

"Dealing with parents is never easy," Hunter said.

"Later, when everything is calmed down," she said, "I'll set up a monthly allowance for them to help them over this hump and arrange for them to live in Mitchell's house. I'm never going to live there again and this way it's not vacant."

"I'm proud of you, Lydia."

"Thank you. I don't feel proud."

He slipped an arm around her and kissed her gently on the lips.

"When did you know you loved me?" she asked, cuddling against him.

"The day we went for ice cream in Lake Tahoe."

"Why do you love me? I've been a doormat most of my life."

"You're strong, compassionate and generous. And you're raising your daughter to be just like you."

"You know now, if you're going to be part of this family, Maya is going to insist that you learn to barrel race, too."

"I did buy a horse," he said with a laugh. He kissed her again. "I didn't expect to become a real cowboy."

With her head resting against his shoulder, she could feel the rumble of his laughter against her cheek. "There's a long tradition of black cowboys in the American West. You'll fit right in."

"What do you think now that you've seen the whole house?" Lydia asked her father. They stood in the empty kitchen of the house Lydia had just bought. Maya and Hunter had gone to the barn to look at what changes it would need in order to be safe and secure for the horses waiting for them with Hector Ibarra. Caroline and Miss E. had gone with them. Lydia felt her mother intended to give her father time to say what needed to be said.

"I like it." He gave the room a critical look. "Maya is going to be happy here."

"So will I."

Silence fell between them.

"Your mother and I had a very long talk and I'm grateful for what you've done. I already called that guy and we have an appointment for next Tuesday." Her father looked out patio doors to the pool and the outdoor kitchen.

"He's very good and he'll get you out of your hole. You said *I*. What about Mom?"

"You need to talk to your mom." Absently he opened a cabinet and peered inside. She sensed he had more to say but didn't know how to. Finally he closed the cabinet and turned to her.

"I owe you an apology for throwing you to the wolves."

Like her mother, her father looked defeated. Her instinct was to tell him he didn't have to apologize, but realized he needed to and she would be gracious and accept it. She needed to make peace with her parents for Maya's sake.

"Dad, I know you've always wanted what was best for me. But I know what's best for me, too."

"And I'm beginning to learn that." He leaned against the counter, the pensive look still on his face. "I know I haven't always been the best of fathers, but I feel like I need to explain."

Lydia waited. She'd never seen her father like this before. He'd been strong, larger than life. Now, he looked old and tired. Lines scored his face. Hair, once black, was now threaded with silver.

"I know your mom and I have never spoken about our background, but I think you should know." He paused as though gathering his thoughts. "We both grew up poor in the Ninth Ward. My mother was the only one of her siblings who had a high school diploma, yet she took in laundry and worked in this big house in the Garden District cleaning. I never knew my dad. He was gone by the time I was born. My mother worked herself to death. By the time I was ten I knew I wanted out of the Projects. And I was prepared to do whatever it took." He paused again, his eyes staring at the past with sadness. "I worked hard, saved every penny because I wanted an education. I worked three jobs to get myself through school and your mother did the same thing. She wanted what I wanted."

Her mother worked. Lydia almost didn't believe him. "Dad," Lydia said. "You don't have to tell me this."

"Yes, I do. The day we left, we never looked back. And every action after that was one more step up the ladder for us, one more barrier between us and the Ninth Ward. We found this falling down, old house and bought it. I worked construction during the day and at night we rebuilt the house from the inside out. Your mother worked as hard at it as I did. We were both pretty surprised when we sold it for almost double what we paid for it. And that was how I got started in real estate. We took the money and bought another old, falling down house in a nice neighborhood, rebuilt it from the inside out and sold that one at a nice profit, too."

"I'm kind of having a hard time picturing you with a hammer in your hand, Dad." Lydia tried to build the image in her mind, but nothing came.

He spread his fingers out. "I had calluses on my calluses."

"What happened to that man who flipped houses?"

He shrugged. "I'm not sure, but at some point the jobs started to fall in my lap. Rich folks wanted me to renovate their falling down homes and then I met Mitchell, who asked if I would be interested in developing some land he had. I said yes and that's when I made my first million and then you were born. After that I had to make more money to keep us all safe. To make sure we didn't end up back in the ghetto. And your mother believed in me through thick and thin." He sighed. "I don't know when making money became more important than being a caring father. I knew someday you'd grow up and marry. I wanted a man who would be rich enough to protect you forever. Mitchell fit the bill. He'd always thought you a pretty little thing."

"You knew Mitchell before I was even born." Mitchell had never told her he'd known her when she was still a baby.

"We didn't see each other often. After I built all the houses he wanted, we went in different directions. We didn't hook up again until you were in college and by that time he was divorced and looking for a second wife."

She remembered that day. Mitchell had been standing against the living room window looking very handsome. He'd taken her hand and kissed it in an old world gesture.

"You think all I worried about was money. Having money meant you didn't have to take in laundry, or work three jobs after school, or eat mayonnaise sandwiches. Money meant safety."

Lydia heard laughter. She glanced out the window and saw Maya with Hunter and Miss E. standing at the edge of the pool.

"Money means choices," Lydia said quietly. She'd never really thought about money before. She'd always had money, like having air to breathe. She didn't know the panic of being without. She studied her dad. She understood that her father was protecting her, but in doing so, he'd stepped hard on her toes and taken away her choices.

"Can you forgive me?"

"I understand that you did what you thought you needed

to keep me safe. You acted out of love. There's nothing to forgive."

"Thank you." He studied his hands as though looking for those calluses he'd talked about.

Lydia watched him. He had a lot of courage. She knew his confession had not been easy. She wanted to hug him, but knew she couldn't quite do that yet. He'd made the first move to mend the fence between them; the next step was up to her.

"Tell me about your young man. Hunter," he said.

"I love him. I didn't want to. Being independent was very important to me, but he sneaked up on me." She laughed a little.

"If it makes you feel any better, I knew the moment I first spotted your mom. She was only thirteen, but from that moment no other woman existed for me."

"At first I worried because I didn't know if I wanted to fall in love with him because he'd take care of me, or fall in love with him because he was the right man for me." Mitchell had been the right man for her for who'd she been at the time. She'd always be grateful to him for preparing her for life after him, forcing her to learn how to handle her and Maya's money. He'd helped her overcome her inherent shyness. He'd given her Maya. That one thing would indebt her to Mitchell for the rest of her life. She didn't realize the huge impact he'd had on her until after he'd passed away, which made her feel sad because she hadn't appreciated him enough until it was too late to tell him.

She sighed.

"What's wrong?" her father asked.

"I was just thinking about Mitchell and how much I appreciated everything he did for me. I never had a chance to tell him."

Her father smiled. "He knew, Lydia. He knew."

"How do you know?"

Her father grinned. "One night he had a little too much bourbon and told me that you and Maya were the best things that ever happened to him."

"He did?"

"He did." Andrew patted her on the shoulder. "He loved you. Very much."

Lydia smiled. "I loved him."

The patio door slid open and Maya bounced into the room. "Mom. Mom, I saw a peacock. Our neighbor over there has peacocks, ostriches and even a llama. Can I have a llama?"

"No," Lydia said with a laugh. "Llamas spit."

"Mr. Hunter said you'd say no."

"Hunter's a smart man," Lydia said with a laugh. She smiled at Hunter as he and his grandmother walked into the kitchen. Caroline stayed behind at the outdoor kitchen opening cabinets and checking out the grill.

"I think I'll go see what my mother is doing," Lydia said. She grinned happily at Hunter, who was being tugged at by Maya, who wanted to show him her bedroom.

"Do you like the house?" Lydia asked her mother. Through the open patio doors her father and Miss E. were talking.

"Once you put your stamp on it, it will be perfect," her mother replied. She sat down on a patio chair and gazed at the pool, her face pensive.

Lydia leaned against the counter. "Dad said you wanted to talk to me."

"Your dad is leaving for New Orleans tomorrow. I'm not going." Caroline plucked nervously at the fabric of her light blue pants.

Surprised, Lydia tilted her head to study her mother. "Why?"

For a long moment, Caroline said nothing. Then she looked up at her daughter. "When I married Andrew, we had nothing except a determination to get out of where we were. Sometimes I felt the only thing that kept us going was because we were a team." She smiled sadly. "Every decision we made was made to get us as far away from where we started as possible. Once we were out, we never looked back."

"You and Dad have always acted like you were embarrassed by your background. Don't you realize that is what made you strong?"

"I never thought of it that way. We thought we were giving you more options and then we started making the choices for you."

"There is the irony of that," Lydia replied.

"Then Andrew started making decisions for me and I just let him even though I resented it at first. This is why I'm not going back to New Orleans. I think we need time apart. I'm hoping you will allow me to stay with you while we work things out between us."

"Are you thinking of a divorce?" Lydia said, alarmed.

"I don't know. It is an option, but not one I want to think about right now. I'm so proud of you and a bit envious."

"Envious of what?"

"You are having this incredible adventure and I'm on the sidelines when I want to be a part of it."

Lydia was too surprised to respond. Her mother, always so prim and proper, was envious of her! "Mom, I would like to have you stay with me, but I think you need to be on your own. I'm sure we can find you a gorgeous little house out here. Or better yet, just stay in my suite at the hotel."

"I've never been on my own."

"Neither was I until after Mitchell passed away. I like it. There is something incredibly empowering about making a decision for yourself, even if it's the wrong one. I'm not sure learning how to ride a horse is my best decision, but I wanted something I could so with Maya that she chose."

"We never gave you that choice," Caroline said sadly. "We put you in situations that were advantageous for us. For that, I'm truly sorry."

Lydia leaned over and gave her mother a kiss on the cheek. "Those things that you did for me made me who I am and I don't regret that. But I want something different for Maya."

"I understand," Caroline said. "I have to find a way to support myself until your father is back on his feet."

Lydia burst out laughing. "You go talk to Miss E. She'll put you to work."

Chapter 13

Hunter set the picnic basket down on the ground. Lydia sat on a rock, her feet dangling in the heated water of the hot strings. He opened the basket and pulled out a bottle of wine and two glasses along with an assortment of cheeses and fruit.

Overhead stars twinkled and a new moon lit the darkness. Lydia wore her bathing suit with a terry cloth robe over it to keep out the chill. Muted sounds from the casino parking lot reached them. Distant music filled the night.

"Maya wants the paint the stable pink. Princess pink." Hunter opened the wine and poured it into the glasses. He handed one glass to Lydia. "And a pink saddle, bridle and reins along with matching pink boots for her."

Lydia sighed. "Pink is her new favorite color. Purple is for babies."

"But a pink stable!" He sat next to her, her closeness a warmth against him.

"Hopefully horses are color blind," Lydia said. "Do you know?"

"Not a clue." He sipped the wine.

She splashed the water with her feet. "My dad left for New Orleans this morning."

"I know. I hear your mother didn't go along." He'd been

so prepared to dislike her parents, and discovering they were just fallible humans had tempered his dislike.

"Apparently, she wants a little *me* time." Lydia nibbled a tiny triangle of brie. "She'll be staying in the hotel for the time being. I'll be moving into my house next week and she'll move into my suite."

"And my grandmother gave her a job." Hunter had been completely caught by surprise at seeing Caroline Fairchild acting as Miss E.'s personal assistant."

"Miss E. will whip her into shape." Lydia chuckled.

"I'm proud of you, Lydia." Seeing her change and grow into her natural strength made him happy. "You've gone through a lot the last couple of days. You outwitted the two stooges, bought two horses, bought a house."

"Fell in love." She gave him a sideways look.

"About that." He pulled a little plastic bubble out of his pocket. He twisted it open and handed her the plastic ring inside with a purple plastic bead in the center. "I won it at Circus Circus when Maya and I were playing some of the games."

"It's lovely." She took the ring and pushed it onto her finger. "Just what I always wanted."

He laughed. "It's a promise ring."

Her eyebrows shot up. "What are you promising?"

"Several things. Number one, you have my heart forever. Number two, I intend to spend the rest of my life making you happy. Number three, when you're ready I want to get married."

"What makes you think I'm not ready now?"

"Because you're still on your grand adventure." He stared at the tacky ring on her finger. "I'm not Mitchell. I'm not going to make decisions for you, or expect you to act a certain way. I need you to be the woman that you are, the captain of your own ship."

She leaned against him. The moonlight lit her face and he saw tears sparkling in her eyes. "Thank you for understanding and your patience."

"I'm having a hard time with the patience part. I can't wait to be Maya's dad." Maya was a bonus. He'd already come to love her as though he were her biological father.

"Maya feels the same way. She's desperate for a father... and brothers and sisters. She's already announced that she wants to teach them all how to ride a horse."

"Miss E. has been talking about great-grandchildren. But not until you're ready." Hunter had never given any thought to children until Maya and knew he wanted at least two more, a little boy that looked like him and another little girl who looked like Lydia.

"Thank you. I'm not ready yet, but I will be. Until that time comes, I want to do something I couldn't do in high school or college."

"And that is?"

"Date. I want to go on dates, have candlelit dinners and go to concerts, and maybe a few more rodeos."

"I can do that." Reno had so much to offer. He'd already thought about expanding his business and Reno had a lot to offer.

"We're going to have so much fun, you and I." Lydia touched his cheek, her fingers warm and inviting.

He grinned. "I know. For the rest of our lives." He kissed her. Her lips were soft, her skin fragrant with the delicate scent of her perfume. He could wait a little bit longer for her. She was worth the wait.

* * * * *

REQUEST YOUR FREE BOOKS!

2 FREE NOVELS
PLUS 2 FREE GIFTS!

KIMANI ROMANCE™

Love's ultimate destination!

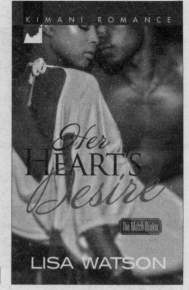